# DEATH ON THE MENU

## THE EB EATS DINER MYSTERIES

## POPPY BRIDGEMAN

Ebook ISBN: 978-1-990509-61-2
Paperback ISBN: 978-1-990509-62-9
Audio book ISBN:978-1-990509-63-6

cover by Getcovers

# FREE BOOK

Claim your copy of Burned by BLT when you sign up for my newsletter learn how Eliza became so determined to clear her name.

# 1

---

I settled into the corner booth, watching Anthone pace between the kitchen and my table like an expectant father. Today was his big test—creating our booth offerings for tomorrow's Charity Food Fair—and he'd been buzzing with nervous energy all afternoon.

"Three dishes, no hidden allergens, and everything has to cost exactly five dollars," I murmured, running through the requirements one more time. Three of those dollars would go to charity, leaving us just two to cover ingredients and our booth fee. Not exactly a recipe for profit, but that wasn't the point. The fair kicked off Nueva Vida's festival season, and Anthone had volunteered to take the lead.

I had to admire his ambition. Most people would have played it safe with standard fair food, but Anthone had spent weeks researching recipes that would stand out from the usual corn dogs and funnel cakes.

The kitchen door swung open with more force than necessary, and Anthone appeared with a plate balanced in one hand and a dish towel slung over his shoulder.

"I've spaced them out so you can taste each one properly," he said, setting the plate down with the careful precision of someone who'd practiced this moment. "Tomorrow they'll be a bit crowded because the fair plates are small."

The aromas hit me first. Garlic and herbs from the bruschetta, the warm spice of the satay chicken, and underneath it all, the tangy heat of buffalo sauce. My stomach reminded me I'd been too busy to eat lunch.

I started with what looked like his take on bruschetta—a thick slice of crusty French bread topped with a perfect slice of tomato and a small ball of bocconcini cheese, the whole thing drizzled with olive oil and balsamic vinegar. Simple, but the flavors were bright and fresh together.

"The tomatoes will be cut to order," Anthone explained, watching my face for any reaction. "But the bread and cheese can be prepped ahead."

Smart thinking. I moved on to the satay chicken—two small skewers with golden-brown meat that smelled like it belonged in a much fancier restaurant than our little diner.

"I can barely tell this isn't peanut sauce," I said after the first bite. The flavor was rich and complex, with just the right amount of sweetness. He'd kept this recipe under wraps the whole time. "What's your secret?"

His face lit up. "Sunflower seed butter instead of peanuts. Same texture, similar taste, but no allergy worries." He gestured toward the skewers. "And see how the chicken slides off easily? I give the bamboo a little twist when I plate it. Nothing worse than having to wrestle your food off a stick."

That attention to the customer experience—that's what would make him successful when he opened his own place. And he would, sooner rather than later, judging by the confidence growing in his voice.

The buffalo wing was my final test. I could feel the heat before it reached my lips, but when I bit into the tender chicken, the spice warmed rather than burned.

"What about people who can't handle any heat?" I asked. Living in New Mexico, you'd think everyone had built up a tolerance, but tourists were a different story. I'd learned that lesson the hard way during my first month.

"Ranch dressing on the side," he said with a grin. "And honestly, if they can't handle this level of spice, they'll probably go for the bruschetta instead."

He had a point. People knew their own limits.

"Okay," I said, pushing the empty plate aside. "I think you're ready."

Anthone slid into the booth across from me, his earlier nervous energy settling into something that looked like relief mixed with excitement.

"Thanks for letting me run with this," he said. "I've been thinking about logistics—we're both going to be on our feet for eight hours straight. Should we ask for a volunteer to help?"

I'd wondered when he'd get to this. The diner would stay open during the fair for customers who preferred sitting down to wandering around with paper plates, which meant we'd be pulled in two directions.

"Who did you have in mind?"

"Maybe Lissa? She's always looking for extra hours."

"Ask her," I said. "But remember, it's volunteer work. Don't pressure her just because she's young and energetic."

I wasn't going to solve this problem for him. Anthone wanted to prove he could handle real responsibility, and that meant making the hard decisions himself. Even the ones about managing people.

"You're going to do great," I told him. "Just make sure you get some sleep tonight. You'll need the stamina."

He laughed and reached for the last wing bone on the plate. "Are you calling me old?"

"Exactly the opposite. You're young enough to think you can handle anything." I stretched, feeling the familiar ache in my lower back that came from a day on my feet. "Trust me, smiling and serving customers is exhausting enough during a regular shift. Tomorrow you'll be doing it for eight hours, mostly with strangers who'll want to chat about every ingredient."

"Yes, ma'am. I'll be here at six to prep, then head over to set up the booth."

The fair officially started at noon, but this was Nueva Vida. "More or less" was about as precise as most schedules got around here, which worked fine for everyone except the tourists who expected things to run like clockwork.

"Mind if I come help with setup?" I asked.

His smile told me I'd walked right into his trap. "I can handle most of it, but if you could clean up after the prep work, Jacquie won't spend the whole day reminding me that I used every pot in the kitchen."

Fair enough. I actually enjoyed the methodical work of cleaning—there was something satisfying about restoring order after creative chaos.

"Try to contain the mess," I said. "I'll be here around eight."

He thanked me and headed back to the kitchen with the plate, and I heard him tell Jacquie that everything had gone according to plan. Their shared laughter made me smile.

I stayed in the booth for another few minutes, watching the late afternoon light slant through the windows and listening to the comfortable sounds of my kitchen prepping for the dinner crowd. Tomorrow would bring its own challenges, but right now, everything felt exactly as it should.

One day of working the fair wouldn't kill me. And there was always ibuprofen.

## 2

The lunch rush had been steady but different today —most of my regulars were busy preparing their own booths for tomorrow's fair. The Catholic church ladies had been in earlier, arguing good-naturedly about whether their famous cinnamon rolls or the Baptist church's peach cobbler would draw bigger crowds. A couple of local artisans had stopped by for coffee to go, their hands already stained with clay and paint, and Will had mentioned that several tribal artists would be displaying pottery alongside the food vendors.

Not just a food fair, then. It made sense to give tourists something interesting to browse between tastings, but it also meant more competition for attention. As my first real foray into Nueva Vida's community events, this was turning out to be bigger than I'd expected.

Anthone was officially in charge of our booth, but everyone would judge EB Eats by how we performed. The thought made my stomach flutter in a way that had nothing to do with hunger.

I was wiping down the counter for the third time when

my mind wandered to the list of upcoming festivals Kashvi had shown me last week. The Charity Food Fair was just the season opener—after this came hot air balloon rides, local brewery and winery tastings, a music festival, and a series of art workshops. The whole thing stretched through fall, designed to bring tourist dollars to Nueva Vida when the summer crowds started thinning out.

I'd been trying to figure out which events I could participate in without burning myself out completely. The hot air balloon rides looked tempting, even if the thought of floating hundreds of feet above the ground made my palms sweaty.

"You look like you're far away from here," Vic's voice cut through my daydream.

"Guilty," I said, dropping the cloth into the cleaning bucket under the counter. Heat crept up my neck—caught woolgathering like a teenager. "Lunch?"

Vic Simons was a firefighter and one of the two men I was currently... well, I wasn't sure what to call it. Dating seemed too strong a word for one interrupted dinner with each of them, but friendship felt too casual for the way my pulse quickened when either of them walked through my door.

"No, just checking on you for tomorrow," he said, holding up a clipboard. "Official fair business. Any last-minute changes to your equipment requests?"

Anthone and I had gone over that list so many times I could probably recite it in my sleep. It would be strange working with just hot plates and portable warmers instead of my familiar kitchen setup. And cooking outside meant dealing with competing aromas from every other booth, not like here where I could almost tell time by the scents drifting from Jacquie's domain.

I glanced at his clipboard but caught myself before taking it from his hands. This was Anthone's test, not mine.

"Anthone," I called toward the kitchen. "Vic needs final sign-off on the equipment list."

The two men moved to the far end of the counter, and I tried not to eavesdrop as they worked through the details. Part of me wanted to hover and double-check everything, but that wasn't the point of this exercise. Anyone could manage when everything went perfectly—the real test was how Anthone would handle problems on his own.

The door chime interrupted my internal pep talk, and I looked up to see Detective George Kramer walking toward the counter. He was the other half of my complicated romantic situation, though calling it a situation might be giving it too much credit.

"Kramer," Vic said without looking up from his clipboard.

"Simons," George replied with equal coolness.

Their mutual chill had nothing to do with me and everything to do with some disagreement about jurisdiction during an arson investigation last year. From what I'd pieced together, both men had valid points, but neither seemed interested in backing down. I kept hoping they'd work it out —having the fire department and police at odds struck me as a recipe for trouble in a town this size.

"Are you here about the fair?" I asked George as he settled onto a counter stool.

"No major issues yet," he said, accepting the coffee I placed in front of him. "Everyone's doing their best to make it work. For us, it's more community relations than law enforcement—not the first event we've handled."

George had been working hard to earn respect from the locals ever since he'd transferred back from Santa Fe. The fact that he'd been born here didn't seem to matter to anyone—he was still the outsider brought in to replace their familiar sheriff—who was sitting in prison because of the bribes and favors he did in office. The way George and his partner worked the murder from a few months back hadn't helped his reputation, and that probably would gone unsolved if Kashvi, Jet, and I hadn't gotten the gossip needed to close it.

"Late lunch?" I asked, watching him add enough sugar and cream to turn his coffee the color of wet sand.

"I have to get back soon," he said, stirring methodically.

"You know, if you like sweet hot milk that much, I could just make you some," I teased. "Might taste better than whatever that is."

He grinned, and for a moment the serious detective facade slipped. "I like the coffee part. You make a good cup, and I'm not a kid who needs hot chocolate."

Fair enough. One of my few firm rules was that customers got their food the way they wanted it, whether that meant well-done steak or coffee that looked more like dessert.

"I could put that in a to-go cup if you're in a hurry," I offered.

"No, I'll drink it here."

I glanced over at Vic and Anthone, still deep in discussion about tomorrow's setup. The equipment list couldn't be that complicated—was Vic stalling until George left? Was George lingering until Vic finished his business? And he'd said he wasn't a kid.

"Slow day for crime?" I asked over the sound of Jacquie scraping down the flat-top grill. The aroma of seared meat and fried onions drifted over us, making my stomach growl.

"Actually, I came to ask you something," George said,

finishing his coffee in one long swallow. "There's an art show opening in a couple of days. Would you like to go?"

An art show. I'd been expecting any dates with George to involve dinner and conversation about police work—somehow I hadn't pictured him as the gallery type.

"That sounds interesting," I said, surprised by how much I meant it. "Yes, I'd love to go."

George nodded and stood, leaving a few bills on the counter. He walked past Vic with a brief nod, and I caught the slight tension in both men's shoulders as they acknowledged each other.

Vic finished up with Anthone and headed for the door, clipboard in hand. "See you tomorrow, Eliza. Should be a good day for it."

After they'd both left, I stood there wondering what I'd gotten myself into. A date a food fair where my reputation was on the line, and enough community politics to make my head spin.

At least I hadn't promised to ride in any hot air balloons. Yet.

## 3

The dinner rush had faded to a comfortable murmur, leaving me with just two lingering customers. Alf Dooken sat in his usual corner booth, making his slice of peach pie last as long as possible while he read through what looked like Lion's Club meeting minutes. Across the diner, Norma Jackson picked at her pie with the careful precision of someone who wasn't really hungry but didn't want to go home to an empty house.

Alf had been my unofficial matchmaker since the day I opened, constantly trying to set me up with what he claimed was an endless supply of eligible relatives. He'd backed off once word got around that both Vic and George were interested, but I still caught him sizing up any single woman who walked through my door.

Norma was harder to read—she'd started coming in more regularly since we'd met and I learned that her wife died, but we'd never talked about her loss directly. I figured sometimes pie was the best therapy I could offer.

Will approached the counter where I was sorting through the day's receipts, already thinking ahead to the end-of-night tally. He grabbed a handful of napkins and started rolling silverware, but something about his posture seemed off. Usually he worked with the easy confidence of someone who'd found his groove, but tonight he moved with the careful deliberation of someone working up to a difficult conversation.

"I heard you and Anthone were thinking about getting some help for tomorrow's booth," he said, not quite meeting my eyes.

My protective instincts kicked in immediately. Will had been clean of gang involvement for over a year now, but I still watched for signs of trouble. If he needed extra hours, I'd find a way to help him out—that was just good business and better humanity.

"Anthone mentioned looking for a volunteer," I said carefully. "You interested in pulling a double shift?"

"Not me. I'm already working here, plus helping set up the pottery display." He'd been connecting with his Apache heritage more over the past few months, and I was glad to see him finding that part of himself. "But Cassidey could use the chance. Not paid work, but something to put on applications. Show she's reliable."

Cassidey. I should have seen this coming. Will's girl-friend—though he'd never officially announced that—was still trying to extract herself from the gang life that had swallowed her up when she was barely more than a kid. Every time she came into the diner, she looked like she was carrying the weight of the world on shoulders that were too thin to bear it.

"That's Anthone's call," I said, not wanting to undermine his authority. "You know why he's running the booth."

"But would you be okay with her? Like, give her a recom-mendation if she does well?" He finished with the silverware and reached for a cleaning cloth, still not quite looking at me.

"Does she have any food service experience?" It was one thing to give someone a chance in my diner where Jacquie and I could keep an eye on things, but the fair would be chaos—no place for on-the-job training.

"Nothing official. That's part of how the gang got her in the first place—no job history, no family support, no one to help her get started on anything legitimate."

The familiar ache settled in my chest. I'd seen Cassidey come in looking half-starved often enough that Jacquie and I had an unspoken agreement to make sure she got a solid meal whenever she showed up. Being sixteen and completely alone was hard enough without having to navigate gang politics for basic survival.

"Everything's prepped and ready for tomorrow," Anthone announced as he emerged from the kitchen, wiping his hands on a paper towel. His voice carried the satisfaction of someone who'd spent hours perfecting every detail.

I caught Will's eye and nodded toward Anthone.

I busied myself cleaning the counter and processing Norma's payment while half-listening to Will make his pitch. His approach was smart—he wasn't asking for charity, just a chance for the girl to prove herself.

"She wouldn't handle any food," Will said. "Just bring people to the booth, maybe work the cash box. You need someone doing crowd control anyway."

Anthone looked at me with the expression of someone who wanted guidance but knew he shouldn't need it. "Eliza, what do you think?"

I'd been turning it over in my mind while I worked. The truth was, if we didn't give Cassidey this chance, who would? Nueva Vida was small enough that word traveled fast—if she couldn't get a reference from the diner, other business owners would notice.

"It would be good to have someone dedicated to customer service," I said, choosing my words carefully. "Give us a chance to focus on the food." If Anthone was going to run his own restaurant someday, he needed to learn how to make these judgment calls.

"Why didn't she come ask herself?" Anthone pressed. "Is she actually interested, or is this your idea?"

Both Will and I could tell from his tone that he was leaning toward yes—he just needed to feel confident about the decision. He'd use this experience over the years because kitchen staff came from all backgrounds.

"She's outside," Will admitted. "I told her I'd ask first, but she'd have to talk to you directly if you were interested."

Alf interrupted the moment by stopping at the counter to pay his bill. "That young lady outside looking for a date?" he asked, glancing toward the window. "I might have a nephew—"

"She's here about work, Alf," I said quickly, not wanting to add matchmaking pressure to an already delicate situation.

Will headed outside to get Cassidey while I wondered, not for the first time, whether Alf's relatives appreciated his enthusiastic efforts on their behalf.

Jacquie appeared at the kitchen window with perfect timing, sliding a grilled cheese sandwich onto the pass. "Figured she might be hungry," she said quietly, and I felt a surge of affection for my cook's intuitive kindness.

I settled into the booth across from where Anthone sat, letting him take the lead while my heart tried to override my business sense. He was much more professional than I would have been—I'd have said yes immediately and worried about the details later.

"This is going to be hard work," he told Cassidey as she slid into the booth, eyeing the sandwich with poorly concealed hunger. "Eight hours on your feet, dealing with crowds, staying pleasant even when customers get cranky."

"I can do that," she said, taking a careful bite of the sandwich as if she was afraid it might disappear. "I've had plenty of practice keeping difficult people happy. With the gang, you learn to stay sweet so you don't get hurt."

The casual way she mentioned violence made my stomach clench, but Anthone pressed on with his questions about customer service and reliability. She answered each one earnestly, promising she'd be on time, work hard, do whatever needed doing.

"Meet us at the fairgrounds at nine," he said finally.

Cassidey's whole face lit up with a smile that made her look like the teenager she really was. "I promise I won't let you down. I'll work really hard, I swear."

After she left, clutching the remaining half of her sandwich, Anthone and I sat in the quiet diner for a moment.

"Think we made the right call?" he asked.

"I think," I said, watching through the window as Cassidey walked away with more spring in her step than I'd ever seen from her, "that sometimes you have to take a chance on people."

He nodded, understanding passing between us. Tomorrow would be a test for all of us—but maybe that was exactly what we all needed.

## 4

Anthone pulled out a small notebook and jotted down a few final thoughts, his brow furrowed in concentration. Even after all our planning, he was still fine-tuning details.

"I hope Cassidey works out," he said, joining me at the counter. "I really want us to sell out—raise as much money as possible for the shelter. Having someone dedicated to drawing in customers could make all the difference."

He was right. With Cassidey handling the crowd and the cash box, we could both focus on food service without constantly stopping to wash our hands between handling money and plates. My body was already protesting the thought of nine hours in the heat—no need to add the punishment of constant hand washing to the mix.

"We'll both be there to make sure she's doing well," I said. "And if she does a good job, we can give her an honest recommendation. Getting legitimate work experience might be the first real step toward leaving the gang behind."

Anthone nodded, but before we could discuss it further, the door chime announced another last minute customer.

Vic walked in, and I felt that familiar flutter of awareness. Seeing him twice in one day was definitely a treat.

"You head home and get some rest," I told Anthone. "We can handle closing up."

Whatever brought Vic in would be our last order, which meant Jacquie could start her kitchen cleanup while Will and I managed the front.

"Dinner?" I asked. "You don't usually stop by after the afternoon rush."

He flashed me that warm, slightly mischievous grin that never failed to make my pulse quicken. The late afternoon sun slanted through the windows, casting everything in golden light that seemed to gather around him like he was posing for some romantic movie poster. The spell broke when Jacquie's sharp voice cut through my daydreaming.

"Order fast if you want food," she called from the kitchen. "Closing everything down in ten minutes."

She'd stay open as long as necessary—Jacquie was nothing if not accommodating—but I appreciated her pushing the evening along. Anthone wasn't the only one who needed to conserve energy for tomorrow. The thought of standing all day in the heat, smiling and serving samples to an endless stream of tourists, made me grateful I wasn't twenty anymore.

"No food," Vic called back to her. "Coast is clear if you want to start shutting down."

So he'd come by just to talk to me? I wasn't ready for a serious relationship, but I'd be lying if I said the special attention didn't make me feel a little giddy. I settled onto one of the counter stools and patted the one beside me.

"Just a chat, then?"

He pulled two name tags on green lanyards from his jacket pocket. "Actually, I forgot to drop these off earlier. All the vendors are supposed to wear them tomorrow." He handed them across to me.

"I need one more," I said, tucking them into my apron pocket. "We added Cassidey to the team—she'll be handling customer service and the cash box."

Vic rubbed his forehead with the heel of his hand. "There's already a mile-long list of people wanting extra tags. Alistair decided at the last minute that his servers should help out. The local tribal council didn't know who'd be working their booth, so they want blanks they can fill in themselves."

I could see the frustration building in his shoulders. Event coordination wasn't exactly the same skill set as fighting fires, and dealing with creative types who changed their minds every five minutes had to be its own special kind of torture.

"If it's easier, we could just take a blank," I offered, pouring him coffee in a to-go cup. "Might be simpler than trying to track down everyone who wants changes. Less printing and delivering for you."

"I'll make one specifically for Cassidey," he said, accepting the coffee gratefully. "But you're right about the blanks. I could give everyone a few extras and let them sort it out themselves."

"Glad I could solve at least one of your problems," I said. "I'm sure you'll have the whole system perfected by next year."

He groaned dramatically. "There won't be a next year. At least not with me in charge. It's bad enough dealing with last-minute changes, but working with people I barely know makes everything ten times harder."

George? Was this his diplomatic way of saying he didn't want to work with his jurisdictional rival?

"Don't give me that look, Eliza. It's not George—we keep things professional. I'm talking about people like Alistair McKay. He doesn't want the responsibility of organizing anything, but he can't let a single decision pass without offering his lengthy, completely useless input on why we're doing it wrong."

I couldn't help laughing at the mental image of Alistair holding court, pontificating about proper fair management to anyone who'd listen. "It's only one more day," I reminded him. "You have a whole year to figure out how to pass the torch to someone else."

He drained his coffee cup, and I gestured toward the pot, offering a refill.

"I've had more caffeine than any human should consume in one day," he said. "Need to get some sleep so I don't collapse tomorrow. Actually, I had two reasons for stopping by."

I slipped the name tags into my pocket and waited for him to continue. Jacquie had called Will into the kitchen, and I could hear the familiar sounds of closing—dishes clattering into the washer, the hiss of cleaner hitting the flat-top grill.

"I need something to help me get through tomorrow," Vic said, raising an eyebrow with that slow grin that made my knees feel unreliable. "If I knew I had a date to look forward to, it might make dealing with Alistair's commentary a little more bearable."

The flutter in my chest intensified. I'd already said yes to George's art show invitation, and Kashvi would never let me hear the end of it if she thought I was playing favorites. Plus, the sudden silence from the kitchen told me our conversation had an audience.

But honestly? A date with Vic would never feel like a chore.

"I'd like that," I said. "Maybe give us both a few days to recover from tomorrow? How about sometime next week?"

"Perfect." He stood and called his thanks to Jacquie and Will before heading for the door.

I locked up behind him and grabbed a cleaning cloth, trying to ignore the knowing looks I was getting from the kitchen. Two dates scheduled in a single day—what had I gotten myself into?

At least I'd have the food fair to distract me from overthinking it. Assuming we all survived tomorrow in one piece.

## 5

"We might run out of food again," Anthone said, his grin so wide it was practically splitting his face. "Cassidey's been incredible at drawing people to the booth. We've already raised more money than I dared hope for."

His enthusiasm was infectious, and I found myself grinning back despite the ache building in my feet. We'd been serving nonstop since ten this morning, and he'd already made two trips back to the diner to restock our supplies. The energy around the fairgrounds was electric—every booth seemed to be doing steady business, and the aroma of different foods mingled in the warm air like some kind of culinary symphony.

Looking around at the crowds, I revised my earlier estimate of the charity's take. When George had mentioned the raffle prizes—a thousand for first place, five hundred for second, two fifty for third—they'd sounded generous. But watching the steady stream of five-dollar transactions at every booth, I suspected we'd already raised close to twenty thousand dollars from all the sales. The raffle winners would get their prizes, but the real winner would be the homeless shelter.

Cassidey appeared at my elbow, digging into her apron pocket and pulling out a thick wad of five-dollar bills. She fed them into our cash box with practiced efficiency.

"People are going crazy for the satay," she said, grabbing a fresh pad of receipts. "Maybe you should let Anthone add it to the menu as a special?"

Watching her work today had been like seeing a flower bloom in fast-forward. This morning she'd been hesitant and jumpy, constantly looking over her shoulder like she expected trouble. Now she moved with confidence, her whole face lit up with genuine happiness. This was prob-ably who she'd always been underneath—before life got complicated, before the gang became her only option for survival.

"I agree completely," I said. "He's earned the right to experiment with the menu. It takes a lot to shine in this industry." The words came out clumsier than I'd intended, and I saw Cassidey's expression shift slightly. "Sorry, I didn't mean that to sound like—"

She burst into laughter, a sound like silver bells that made her look even younger than her sixteen years. "I know what you meant. But I am going to work really hard for that reference you promised me. I want to earn a good one." She tucked the receipt pad into her apron and straightened her shoulders. "Gotta run—lots of hungry people to tempt over here."

She wasn't wrong about hungry. I'd noticed several customers making second and third rounds, sampling favorites from different booths. The festival had drawn what looked like several thousand people, mostly tourists with that slightly overwhelmed expression of people trying to see everything at once.

"They come for the whole season," said Woody Howell, shuffling up to our booth his careful gait that protected his aging knees. "Tours, some of them organized by June Spenser. People plan two-week vacations around all the different events."

I handed him his passed over a sample plate of satay, trying to process this information. "When do they usually arrive? I haven't noticed a big uptick in diner traffic."

Woody picked up one of the satay skewers and examined it like a scientist studying a specimen. "Most of them got in this morning. The tour packages are designed to fit a normal vacation schedule—most folks can't take more than two weeks off work. All the festivals got squeezed into that window." He took a careful bite and nodded approvingly. "Jet's got a group over at the pottery display right now. Nice work on this recipe, by the way."

He wandered off toward Pearl's bakery stall, where she was offering tiny samples of cookies and cupcakes. Her business looked just as brisk as ours, partly because Cassidey had been steering people in her direction for dessert. That girl definitely had a future in sales if she could stay out of trouble long enough to build on it.

A woman with a teenage boy approached and took my last satay plate. Anthone was refilling the supplies as fast as he could, but keeping up with the demand seemed a task beyond anyone.

"Are you absolutely sure this is allergy-free?" she asked, holding up the satay skewer. "I know you said no peanuts, but my son is deathly allergic and I always double-check everything."

I assured her that we'd used sunflower seed paste

instead of peanuts and that no peanut products had come anywhere near our preparation area. She thanked me and walked away, handing one skewer to her son and working the chicken off the other.

"You're letting that little criminal handle your cash box?" The voice behind me dripped with disdain, and my heart sank. I'd been hoping to avoid this particular confrontation all day.

Alistair McKay stood there with his arms crossed, looking like he'd been personally insulted by our success. His own booth at the far end of the row looked considerably less busy than most of the others.

"Cassidey's doing an excellent job," I said evenly. "Have you tried our sample plate?"

He sneered at the food I offered, though it looked just as appealing now as it had this morning. The aroma of vinegar and spices from the buffalo wings was making my own mouth water.

"I can't believe anyone would want to mix those flavors," he said with a dismissive wave. "Cheese and hot sauce? And that satay definitely has peanuts in it. You should have a warning sign up."

I bit back the urge to explain Anthone's brilliant substitution. If Alistair wasn't going to try the food, he could stay ignorant about our ingredients. The less he knew about our methods, the better.

"How are things going at your booth?" I asked, hoping he'd take the hint and return to his own business.

"I've got one of my servers running it," he said, glancing over his shoulder toward the Dunes stall. "I'm sure we'll bring in far more than you. Everyone wants comfort food—tomato soup and grilled cheese."

In this heat? I doubted it, but I just wanted him gone.

Behind him, I could see Cassidey making subtle gestures, clearly frustrated that his negative energy was driving potential customers away from our area.

"Well, I'm sure she could use your help," I said. "It's hard to manage crowds like this when you're working alone."

That finally got him moving, but not before he shot one more disapproving look at our setup.

Cassidey slipped up beside me as soon as he was out of earshot. "Julie looks miserable over there," she said quietly. "I've been sending people to the Dunes booth because I feel bad that she's not getting many customers. Should I stop?"

"No, keep doing that," I said, trying to get a better look at Alistair's offering. "This is all for charity—the more money everyone raises, the better."

"Don't bother looking," Cassidey said with a grimace. "It's lukewarm soup in little cups and greasy squares of grilled cheese on sticks. Is there anything we can do to help her, or should I get back to work?"

Anthone placed the last sample plate on our counter and turned to Cassidey. "Actually, could you run back to the diner and grab that final box of prepped food? We're almost cleaned out."

She practically bounced with excitement at being trusted with the task. "Be right back!"

"I didn't realize how young she really is until today," Anthone said, watching her weave through the crowd with new energy. "She usually looks so worn down. It ages her about ten years."

"Glad you decided to give her this chance?" I asked, though I already knew the answer. Seeing him learn to be a generous employer would serve him well when he opened his own place.

"Enough that I think you should consider hiring her," he

said, handing out sample plates with practiced efficiency. "She's got real potential."

"I don't know if the budget can handle another employee right now," I admitted. "But let me run the numbers tonight. Maybe a trainee position?"

Before he could respond, a high-pitched scream cut through the cheerful festival noise like a knife, freezing everyone within a hundred yards.

The charity fair had just taken a very dark turn.

## 6

I froze for a heartbeat, my sample plate forgotten in my hands. This wasn't the joyful shriek of a child spotting the face-painting booth, or even the frustrated wail of a toddler who'd been denied a third cookie. I'd heard plenty of both throughout the day. This was something else entirely—raw shock and terror that cut through the festival chatter like a blade.

I shoved my plate at Anthone and scanned the crowd until I spotted Cassidey standing motionless near the pottery display, her face turned toward the sound.

"Make sure Cassidey's okay," I told Anthone. "I'll go see if someone needs help."

He nodded and called the girl over while I pushed through the clusters of confused fairgoers. Everyone had stopped what they were doing, conversations dying mid-sentence as people tried to figure out what had happened.

I headed toward the open square at the end of our row, where picnic tables were scattered for people who preferred to sit while they ate. The tables were usually occupied by elderly visitors and families with small children—people who needed a break from wandering the booths with paper plates in hand.

A crowd was already forming around the first table, drawn by that horrible combination of curiosity and dread that accompanies any crisis. A woman stood with both hands pressed over her eyes, as if she could unsee whatever had made her scream. At her feet, another woman lay motionless on the ground beside an overturned chair.

I pushed through the gathering onlookers, thinking about crime scene contamination. Even if this turned out to be a medical emergency rather than something sinister, the police wouldn't appreciate having evidence trampled by curious bystanders.

"Is there a doctor here?" I called out, kneeling beside the fallen woman. "Has anyone called 911?"

"I did," June Spenser said, holding up her phone like proof of citizenship. "Left Jet in charge of the pottery tour when I heard the screaming."

I pressed my fingers to the woman's neck, searching for a pulse while trying not to disturb her position. Her skin felt cool despite the afternoon heat, and I couldn't find any sign of life. If she'd collapsed from heat exhaustion or a heart attack, we were already too late to help her.

"Please step back," George's familiar voice cut through the crowd noise, and I looked up to see him approaching with two uniformed officers.

"Keep everyone back," he instructed them. "And contact Detective Collett. Tell her we need her here now."

He knelt beside me and lowered his voice. "What happened?"

"I can't find a pulse," I said quietly. "But I'm not exactly qualified to make that determination."

He gave me a look that was half exasperation, half affection. "You're not qualified to investigate crimes either, but that doesn't seem to stop you."

"Very funny," I muttered, though I appreciated his attempt to lighten the mood. Gallows humor over an actual body probably wasn't appropriate, but we both needed something to cut through the gravity of the moment.

"I've got Doc Surrey," Vic announced, appearing at George's elbow with the festival's volunteer medical officer. "Ambulance is en route."

George and I moved aside to give the doctor room to work. While Doc Surrey made his examination, George scanned the ground around the table. The picnic area was littered with the detritus of a busy food fair—dropped napkins, empty cups, scattered crumbs, and the occasional chunk of food that hadn't made it to someone's mouth.

Doctor Surrey's assessment was quick and definitive. "She's gone. Looks like a severe allergic reaction—I can smell peanuts on her breath. Want me to turn her over, check for other causes?"

"We'll wait for the medical examiner," George said. "Until then, I'm treating this as a potential crime scene."

My stomach dropped. "How can you be sure it's not just an accident?"

George's expression was grim. "People with life-threatening food allergies are incredibly careful about what they eat. They read every label, ask detailed questions about ingredients. It's possible someone made an honest mistake, but in my experience, that level of carelessness is rare."

He was right, and we both knew it. The woman with the peanut allergy who'd double-checked our satay ingredients flashed through my mind. People who could die from trace amounts of allergens didn't take chances. This wasn't her, thank goodness.

"Go back to your booth, Eliza," George said. "I need to secure this area, and I don't want civilians contaminating potential evidence."

I understood his position, but his tone rubbed me the wrong way. "There's no need to be pushy about it. Our booth followed all the allergen protocols—we can't be responsible for this."

"We'll be coming by to ask questions," he said. "Don't go anywhere."

One of the officers approached and waited for George's attention. I took a step backward, hoping to blend into the crowd. If this turned into another murder investigation—and George's attitude suggested it would—I wanted to gather as much information as possible before I got shut out of the loop.

"Anyone here know this woman?" George called out to the assembled crowd.

Tina Ingles stepped forward, her fluorescent green hair catching the afternoon sunlight. "She's probably a tourist. I don't recognize her, and nobody I've talked to knows her name."

So much for George's attempt at community policing. He was about to discover that giving Nueva Vida's gossip network official permission to help could be either his best decision or his worst nightmare.

"Detective," an officer said, clearly holding information that couldn't wait.

"What do you have, Bowman?"

The officer consulted his notebook. "We searched her purse. Driver's license identifies the victim as Diana Whitfield. She's got five food receipts in her bag, plus one still clutched in her hand. We didn't disturb that one."

"What else?"

"Twenty-three dollars in cash, a roll of antacids, lip gloss, compact mirror, and an unused EpiPen."

An unused EpiPen. If Diana Whitfield knew she had a life-threatening allergy, why hadn't she used her emergency medication? Either she didn't realize what was happening until it was too late, or something had prevented her from reaching it.

"Thanks," George said. "When the medical examiner removes the body, make sure all of that gets logged into evidence."

"Detective Collett has Joey watching the scene. Kid's doing good work for a rookie."

George turned back to me with that familiar look of frustrated authority. "I thought I told you to return to your booth."

"Now that I know her name, I can ask around—see if anyone remembers talking to her," I said. "Let me know when you want to interview us."

I started back toward our booth, my mind already churning through what I'd observed. There wasn't anything more I could do here, but I could start writing down everything I remembered while the details were still fresh.

Alistair McKay pushed past me, heading toward the crime scene with the determined stride of someone who had Important Information to share. His voice carried across the square as he called for George's attention.

"I saw her eating at the diner booth!" he shouted, pointing back at me with dramatic flourish. "You should search there first!"

I shrugged and kept walking. If he was right, my receipt

would be among those found in Diana Whitfield's purse, along with the others. When I got back to the booth, I'd ask Anthone if he remembered her—and hope that whatever she'd eaten from us hadn't been the thing that killed her.

The successful charity fair had just become something much darker, and I had the sinking feeling that EB Eats was about to be at the center of another murder investigation.

## 7

W hen I returned to our booth, Anthone was still serving customers despite the chaos I just left. I had to admire his focus—apparently witnessing a potential murder didn't stop people from wanting lunch.

"What actually happened over there?" he asked, handing out sample plates without missing a beat. "I've heard three different rumors, but I don't know what's true and what's Nueva Vida gossip enhancement."

I realized it had only been about fifteen minutes since the scream. In a town this size, that was barely enough time for the initial shock to wear off, let alone for the full story to make the rounds.

"A woman died," I said quietly, then explained about the apparent allergic reaction and the smell of peanuts. "George will be coming by to take our statements since Alistair announced she eaten here." He could have made up the story, but if so, she wouldn't have one of our receipts.

Anthone's face went pale. "But nobody's supposed to use any kind of nuts in their food today. The rules were crystal clear about that." His voice dropped to a worried whisper. "Do you think I made a mistake somehow?"

"Absolutely not," I said firmly. "But we still need to give statements, and George will want to verify our ingredients." I looked around the booth area, scanning for a familiar figure. "Where's Cassidey?"

He followed my gaze, checking the nearby booths. "She came over for a new receipt pad and went back to selling. She was working the area around the pottery display, bringing people over. Haven't seen her in the last few minutes, but people are still coming with the receipts she gave them."

So she'd been working right up until recently. "I need to find her before she hears rumors and panics," I said. "If she thinks the police are going to question her extensively, she might bolt."

"Yeah, Denise Collett hasn't exactly built a reputation for gentle interrogation," Anthone agreed. "Do we know who died? If she bought food from us, I might remember her."

That reminded me why I'd wanted to talk to him. I kept scanning the crowd for Cassidey while I described Diana Whitfield as best I could remember her.

"She never got a chance to use her EpiPen," I added, watching his face for any recognition.

He absently handed out plates while his mind worked. "Blond, maybe five-foot-four, wearing jeans and a pink t-shirt?" He rubbed his forehead as if trying to massage the memory loose. "Yes, I remember her now. You were talking to Tina Ingles at the time, but she came up and asked to see our ingredient list. Made a point of telling me about her peanut allergy." He paused, thinking. "I remember thinking that if I had a reaction that severe, I'd probably just avoid eating at food fairs entirely. She specifically wanted to try our satay because she could never eat the traditional version."

"So she would have been equally careful at every other booth," I said, still no sign of Cassidey anywhere. Around us, I noticed that business had slowed to a trickle at most booths as word of the death spread. "Unless someone outright lied about their ingredients, this probably wasn't food from the fair at all."

"Or someone made an honest mistake," Anthone said, but I could hear the doubt in his own voice. "It could have been me."

I couldn't let him spiral into self-doubt. "Anthone, you didn't make a mistake. If you can't trust yourself to be careful with something this important, you'll never have the confidence to run your own restaurant."

"I know, and it's not like me to second-guess everything. I guess I'm just rattled that my first big test as a leader might end up connected to a murder."

Murder was George's theory, not confirmed fact, but I had to agree with Anthone's logic. "This will all look different in a few days. And honestly? I'd bet money that the peanut contamination didn't come from any of today's food vendors."

"If people aren't coming around anyway, I should prob-ably store the remaining food back in the cooler," he said, reaching for the sample plates. "Even if business picks up, we've only got a couple more hours before—Cassidey! You scared me."

I leaned over the counter to see her squirming out from underneath, where she'd apparently been hiding the entire time. Part of me understood her fear, but another part felt uncomfortably like I'd been spied on.

I joined them behind the booth counter and poured

glasses of the iced tea we'd brought to stay hydrated. The blend of black tea and orange had just the right balance of bitter and sweet to cut through the afternoon heat and my growing anxiety.

"You heard everything?" I asked after we'd all taken a few sips.

"Can I leave now?" Cassidey asked instead of answering. "I can't talk to the police. If my boss finds out I was answering questions about anything, he'll think I'm giving them information about gang business."

I looked at Anthone, reminding myself that he was in charge today. I couldn't let her disappear—we all knew that —but how he handled this would reveal a lot about the kind of leader he'd become.

"You need to stay," he said gently but firmly. "But we can all take a break until people start thinking more about food and raffle prizes than about crime scene gossip."

She stared at her feet, every muscle in her body coiled like she was about to make a break for it.

"We won't let the police intimidate you," I said quickly. "And think about it—if you run now, your boss will wonder why. If you stick around and answer routine questions, he'll be glad you didn't bring Detective Kramer sniffing around for you."

She looked up at me, taking a deep breath as she processed this logic. "I hadn't thought of it that way. And forget Detective Kramer—what if Detective Collett decides to bring down the hammer?"

Despite everything, she grinned at her own exaggeration, and I had to chuckle. Her body was still tense with fear, but I was relieved that she could see the sense in staying put. As long as she thought like someone trapped in gang life, it would be nearly impossible for her to break free.

"Are you folks still open?" The call came from Brad Vincent, Vic's uncle, holding out a crumpled five-dollar bill. "I'm still eating, and it looks like everyone else is starting to wander back to the food booths too."

Cassidey took his money and handed him a receipt with practiced efficiency. "Don't forget to fill out the back with your name and contact info, then drop it in the raffle barrel."

Anthone passed Brad a sample plate. "Isn't this your second helping today?"

"Sure is. Liked it so much the first time I had to come back for more." He gestured toward Alistair's booth with obvious disdain. "Better than that slop McKay's serving up. This chicken thing is good enough for your regular menu. I'd actually come to the diner if you put it on there."

Coming from Brad, who usually only showed up at EB Eats when Vic drove him in for breakfast, that was high praise. He might be rough around the edges, but I appreciated his straightforward honesty.

"It's Anthone's recipe," I said. "So that's his decision to make."

Brad fixed Anthone with a squinty-eyed stare. "Well? You planning to charge her licensing fees or something?"

Anthone made a show of considering the commercial implications, then laughed. "I guess the recipe belongs as much to Eliza as it does to me. We can fight about the details when I open my own place."

"Good answer," Brad said approvingly. "Now, are you going to investigate this thing, Eliza? You and Kashvi and that tour guide friend of yours?"

"We'll see," I said, not wanting to commit to anything until I'd talked to my unofficial investigation team.

Brad didn't believe my noncommittal response for a

second. He grunted a laugh and headed off with his plate, probably to sample more booths before the fair officially closed.

As I watched him go, I realized he was right—we probably would end up investigating. The question was whether we'd get started before George decided we were interfering with official police business and try to shut us down.

# 8

———

Business had picked up again, not just at our booth but throughout the fairgrounds. I found it oddly unsettling that people could continue eating after a woman had died from food poisoning just yards away. But then again, if you didn't have life-threatening allergies, maybe it felt like someone else's problem—a tragic accident that couldn't possibly happen to you.

About half an hour after I'd returned from the crime scene, our supplies were running dangerously low and we were starting to talk about shutting down early. Based on our sales, I estimated the charity would collect around twelve thousand dollars from the food vendors alone—a substantial windfall for the homeless shelter. Our portion would barely cover our costs, but I assumed that was true for everyone. The raffle prizes were cash off the top, with the grand prize set at a thousand dollars. All in all, it had been a successful fair—if you could overlook the fact that someone had been murdered.

"Can't they just come to the diner to interview us?"

Cassidey asked, and while it wasn't quite a whine, I could hear the exhaustion creeping into her voice. Now that the adrenaline was wearing off, she was feeling every hour we'd spent on our feet. "We could sit down, maybe have some fries. I can pay this time."

I wasn't about to let her spend her money when she'd volunteered her time today, and I had to admit the idea of comfortable chairs and a cold drink sounded appealing. My back was protesting the hours of standing, and my mind kept circling back to the image of Diana Whitfield collapsed beside that picnic table.

"I'm sure they'll get to us soon," I said, though I had no real idea how long police interviews took. "If we leave now, George might decide we need to give our statements at the station instead."

Cassidey huffed and went back to organizing the cash box. "I guess there's still an hour left officially. Maybe we can sell the rest of this stuff after they finish with us."

I wasn't sure anyone would still be hungry enough for samples by then. The day was cooling as afternoon moved toward evening, and I could smell rain in the air—not the sharp, clean scent I remembered from Oregon, but that distinctive summer storm smell, petrichor. Slightly dusty and warm, it reminded me of childhood afternoons when thunderstorms would roll in without warning.

"Here they come," Anthone said, nodding toward the approaching figures of George and Denise. "Cassidey, remember what we talked about—you need to ask for an adult to be present when you give your statement."

"One of you, right?" she asked, separating our earnings into neat piles. "If we have to wait for Social Services, we could be here all night."

"One of us, yes we'll do it if you want, but I also saw Tina Ingles and Norma Jackson still around," I said. "You might be better off with one of them." I wasn't sure if someone who could potentially be a person of interest in the case should serve as a guardian for a witness.

"Fine. Tina's probably the best choice," Cassidey said, placing the money back in the cash box and handing Anthone the key.

"Thanks for waiting," George said as he reached our booth. "We'll be wrapping up the fair soon. Marjorie's taking over the coordination for me—she's collecting receipts from attendees for the raffle right now."

"I need your complete ingredients list and any leftover samples for testing," Denise said, her tone more businesslike than hostile. She handed Anthone a stack of evidence bags. "I'll observe while you pack these, then I'll take your statement."

She and Anthone moved to the back of the booth, leaving me with George and Cassidey. The girl stepped closer to me, clearly seeking the comfort of familiar company.

"What about the cash?" Cassidey asked. "The charity can't wait for you to solve the case to get their money."

George's expression softened into something approaching a smile—a sharp contrast to his partner's professional demeanor. "Marjorie will collect the donation totals as soon as she has all the receipts tallied. It's not like we can trace the killer through DNA on five-dollar bills."

"Wouldn't that make your job easier," I said, hoping to lighten Cassidey's obvious anxiety.

She took a small step back but stayed with us, her body language still tense with barely contained fear.

Denise returned with Anthone and a handful of our remaining samples sealed in evidence bags. "Everything looks consistent," she reported to George. "Unless someone was incredibly careless, this was premeditated."

The word hit me like a cold stone in my stomach. Not just murder, then—not a crime of passion or a moment of anger gone wrong. Premeditated meant someone had planned this, had deliberately set out to kill Diana Whitfield. But if she was a tourist, as Tina suspected, why would anyone in Nueva Vida want her dead? What could a visiting stranger have done to warrant murder?

George turned his attention back to us. "Did any of you see her after she left your booth?"

Anthone nodded. "I handed her the sample plate when she came over. She asked a lot of detailed questions about ingredients, but I guess that makes sense if her allergy was potentially fatal. She left our booth and headed toward the picnic area. I didn't watch her all the way—we were too busy serving other customers."

Good answer. He stuck to the facts without offering speculation, which would help keep the investigation focused. Not that I wanted anything held back from the police, but inconsistencies would just slow down their work.

"Cassidey, do you remember selling her a plate?" Denise asked. She used the girl's first name, which seemed friendly enough, but there was an edge in her tone that I didn't like.

Cassidey looked down at her hands as she spoke. "Lots of people asked about the satay—I guess it's pretty popular since so many people can't eat the traditional version. I think I remember her, but I only really talk to customers until they hand me their money. If it's the same woman I'm thinking of, she came from the direction of the bakery booth. She didn't have a plate in her hand, but I noticed she had a bit of sugar on her lip—probably from Pearl's donuts." She took a deep breath, and I gave her arm a reassuring pat.

"We'll follow up on that," George said. "I'll need complete statements from all of you, but right now it's more important that we collect contact information from as many attendees as possible."

"Yeah, Marjorie's gathering people for the raffle drawing now," Denise added. "I'll get this money to her so she can distribute the prizes. I've told the uniforms to prioritize interviewing tourists first—they might leave town—and make note of locals for follow-up later."

"We should get back to coordinating," George said, nodding toward the evidence bags. "Put those in the trunk with the other samples we've collected. We'll drive everything to the lab as soon as we finish here."

Denise shot a stern look in Cassidey's direction. "We'll be back for your statements."

After they left, I turned to Anthone. "Why don't you go see if you won anything in the raffle? Cassidey, do you have any receipts to enter?"

She jammed her hands deeper into her pockets. "No. I need to keep all my money for... other things."

I wished I'd thought to take her around to sample food from other booths—a small treat after such a long day. But she had her reasons for being careful with money, and those reasons weren't my business. Working with her all day had convinced me she wasn't using drugs, so I kept my opinions to myself.

"If the fair's shutting down early, we should close out our booth now," I said. "Help me with the cleanup, and we can eat some of the leftovers before they go bad."

The temperature was dropping steadily, and when the rain started, it would turn the field into a muddy mess. We weren't responsible for taking down the booth structure, but we could leave everything ready for the cleanup crew.

As I started packing up our supplies, I couldn't shake the feeling that Diana Whitfield's death was just the beginning of something much more complicated than a simple food poisoning case.

## 9

The rain was still holding off, but dark clouds were gathering overhead and I wasn't sure how much longer we could stay. The teardown crew had already started dismantling booths in our row, which meant we'd have no shelter if the weather finally broke.

"I'll start taking statements now," Denise said, appearing beside me so suddenly I nearly jumped out of my skin. "Where's Anthone?"

"He went to watch the raffle drawing," I said, glancing toward the main stage area. "I assume he's still there—I haven't heard any victory shouts yet." I settled my shoulders, preparing for what was probably going to be an uncomfortable conversation. "Why don't you start with me? Though I don't have much to report."

Denise glanced over at Cassidey, who was deep in conversation with Tina Ingles near the pottery display. "Actually, I'll start with the kid."

If it meant Cassidey could go home sooner, I was all for it. "I'll wait here, then."

I watched as Tina immediately stepped into her protective role, positioning herself slightly between Denise and Cassidey. The girl must have filled Tina in on her situation, because the older woman's body language radiated fierce maternal energy. If Denise tried to push too hard or bring up anything gang-related, Tina would shut it down fast.

I didn't even feel excluded from the conversation. Cassidey or Tina would fill me in on anything important later. And since I was determined not to interfere with the official investigation this time, it really didn't concern me. Right?

"Okay, what have you heard?" Jet's voice made me jump for the second time in five minutes. How were people managing to sneak up on me when there was absolutely no cover in this open field?

"Peanut oil, severe allergic reaction, no nuts in any of the food vendors' offerings," I summarized as Kashvi joined us —at least she wasn't trying to be stealthy. "Victim was a tourist named Diana Whitfield."

"That's not much to go on," Kashvi said, pulling out her investigative notebook. "We'll have to work the gossip network hard if we want to get ahead of this."

I'd just finished telling myself we weren't going to investigate this time. "We should stay out of it and let the police handle everything."

"Why is Denise giving Cassidey the third degree?" Jet asked, nodding toward the interview in progress. "Seems to me there are plenty of more likely suspects around here."

I followed his gaze, Tina stood with her arms crossed, not quite blocking Denise's access to Cassidey but clearly ready to step in if needed. Cassidey was looking everywhere except at the detective, her body language screaming discomfort. And Denise was actually pointing a finger in

Tina's face, her voice carrying an edge that made several passersby stop and stare.

I didn't need to join in, Cassidey's chosen protector was doing a great job. "Tina can hold her own," I said, "but if Detective Collett is going to harass Cassidey, then, yes, we need to solve this case quickly."

"Did George mention any other clues?" Kashvi asked, pen poised over her notebook. "We need somewhere to start."

"The victim had five receipts in her purse," I said, pulling the information from my memory of the crime scene. "Our booth, Pan de Vida bakery, Los Amigos taco stand, Frontier Burgers, and Tropical Smoothies. Though that doesn't necessarily mean she only ate from those places —maybe the killer removed an incriminating receipt."

"I don't remember her booking any tours with us," Jet said, "but we're coordinating with all the festival vendors this season. We should talk to the booth owners and workers who served her."

"Tomorrow," I said firmly. "I don't see any way to ask questions without George or Denise catching wind of it."

"I'll get everything organized," Kashvi said, already making notes. "My back room in two hours? The statements should be finished by then, and it gives you time to bring dinner."

"And time to shower and change," I added, suddenly aware of how the day's heat and stress had left me feeling grimy. "Standing in this heat all day isn't exactly a spa treatment."

Kashvi glanced up at the threatening sky and dug into her tote bag, producing two collapsible umbrellas. She pressed them into my hands. "One for you, one for Cassidey.

And if you haven't given your statement in the next half hour, tell George to come find you."

I was grateful for the umbrellas, but holding them while we waited seemed awkward. I set them on the ground and looked up to see Anthone making his way back through the thinning crowd.

"No luck with the raffle prizes, but I got my statement done," he said, slightly out of breath. "I see Denise is working on Cassidey now."

I asked if he'd learned anything new during his interview, but apparently the police were being more efficient and tight-lipped than usual. No gossips allowed, minimal information shared.

"I'll see what I can find out from the other vendors," he offered. "Do you need help with anything right now?"

"We're ready to leave as soon as Denise interviews me," I said, keeping one eye on the tense conversation across the pathway. "Do you need a ride, or are you heading out on your own?"

He looked around the booth area with a frown. "Where are the coolers with our leftover supplies?"

"Already loaded in my car," I said, not wanting to take my attention completely off Cassidey's interview.

"I could take them to the diner and come back to wait with you," he suggested. "Or I could pick up something more substantial than our leftover samples for dinner."

I thought about Kashvi's invitation and our impromptu investigation meeting. "I don't need anything special. Just come back with the car—if I'm not talking to one of the detectives when you return, we'll leave. Cassidey gets dinner on me tonight, and you should give her some cash for her work today."

"I already decided to give her something. I was thinking maybe forty dollars?" he said. "Does that sound fair?"

She wasn't expecting any payment at all, but after her comment about needing to save every penny, I knew the money would be welcome. I nodded approvingly. "Head out now so we're not stuck here all night."

As Anthone walked away, I settled in to wait for my turn with Detective Collett, trying not to worry about what questions she might be asking Cassidey. Despite my best intentions to stay out of police business, it looked like we were about to launch another unofficial investigation.

Some habits, apparently, were harder to break than others.

## 10

Denise closed her notebook with a sharp snap and walked over to me, her expression all business. "You can head back to the diner," she said curtly. "Rain's coming, and we're too busy making sure we can track down all these tourists to take your statement now. Don't leave town. Answer when we call. And stay out of our investigation."

The glare she fixed on me felt like she was trying to brand those last words directly onto my forehead. I managed a polite smile despite the irritation prickling under my skin.

"Thanks for the consideration," I said evenly. "If you're still tied up after the diner closes, just call and I'll let you know where to find me."

I watched her stomp away through the crowd as the first fat raindrops began to fall. Tina reached my side with Cassidey close behind, both of them moving with the urgency of people who knew what rain meant in the high desert.

"I need to get going," Tina said, glancing up at the darkening sky. "Can't risk getting cut off if the creeks start rising. Flash floods earn their name here." She turned to Cassidey, her expression serious. "You tell Eliza everything you know. Even the stuff you held back from that detective. Don't look at me like that—if I could tell you were hiding something, she definitely could. I'm surprised she let it slide."

Despite the stern words, Tina pulled Cassidey into a fierce hug before hurrying toward the parking area.

I handed Cassidey one of Kashvi's umbrellas and we made our way through the mud that was already forming as the rain picked up. Anthone would be back with my car soon.

"You can tell me what Tina meant when we're sitting in a comfortable booth with a hot plate of fries," I said.

"They think I killed her," Cassidey said quietly, not meeting my eyes. "Tina thinks so too, but she was good to have there. Thanks for suggesting her."

The rain was coming down harder now, and she hunched her shoulders against it even though the umbrella was keeping us mostly dry. Whatever she'd held back from Denise, it was clearly weighing on her.

"I don't think you did anything wrong," I said firmly. "Here's Anthone now. Let's get back to EB Eats, and then you can tell me everything."

"Are you guys really going to investigate?" she asked as she climbed into the back seat. "I thought you were going to leave it to the police this time."

"That was before I found out they're treating you as a suspect," I said, settling into the passenger seat as Anthone pulled away from the fairgrounds.

Five minutes later, Cassidey and I were in the corner booth farthest from the door, with the diner almost empty around us. Most of my regulars were probably still being questioned at the fairgrounds, which gave us the privacy we needed for this conversation.

Lissa appeared with two steaming mugs of hot chocolate, the marshmallows already melting into creamy swirls. "Figured you'd need something to warm you up after that weather," she said. "Jacquie's got tomato soup and grilled cheese coming right up. Heard Alistair was serving a terrible version at the fair, so we thought we'd show people how it's really done."

"I think we'll have a while before the dinner rush hits," I said. "But when they come, everyone's going to want food and gossip after what happened today."

"As long as they buy something while they're gossiping," Lissa said with a grin. "It's been dead quiet here all day. So it's really murder, not just an accident?"

Of course Anthone would have filled them in when he dropped off the coolers. The Nueva Vida gossip network was already spinning up to full speed.

"Yes," I said simply. I'd share what I could, but Cassidey was my priority right now.

"I'll keep other customers away from your table as long as possible," Lissa promised. "And if George or Denise show up, I'll try to give you a heads-up."

The service bell chimed, and she hurried off to collect our food from the kitchen pass. I could see Anthone talking to Jacquie, probably sharing more details about the day's events.

I let Cassidey taste her first few spoonfuls before pressing for information. Jacquie's tomato soup was always perfect—bright and complex with just a hint of basil—and the grilled cheese was cut into perfect soldiers for dipping. Comfort food at its finest, which we both needed after the day we'd had.

"Okay," I said when she'd eaten enough to take the edge off her hunger. "Tell me everything. Even what you held back from Detective Collett."

She stirred her soup thoughtfully, not meeting my eyes. "Will you make me tell her everything too?"

"I honestly don't know yet, but probably," I said gently. "Maybe I can arrange for George to handle the follow-up interview instead. Would that be easier?"

I didn't want to scare her into silence, but I couldn't promise to withhold important information from the police. The rain chose that moment to intensify, drumming against the windows and adding to the cozy intimacy of our corner booth.

"I guess it doesn't matter which cop you tell," she said with a resigned sip of hot chocolate. "A cop is a cop." She pushed her half empty bowl away and sat back. "Most of what I told her was true. I do kind of remember selling her the plate, mainly because I wondered why someone so worried about ingredients would risk eating at a food fair in the first place."

I nodded, resisting the urge to interrupt. Without my notebook, I needed to hear the whole story before asking questions—scattered conversations were harder to remember accurately later.

"I don't like people knowing this," she continued, her voice dropping even lower, "but I'm staying at the homeless shelter. I won't give you all the details, but I need a real job and a permanent address. Before I get anything official like a license. If I can rent my own place it's a start. Once I have those, it'll be easier to break away from... everything. Not all of us have family to help out."

I bit back the dozen questions and expressions of sympathy that rose to my lips. She didn't want them, and it wasn't my business unless it became relevant to the investigation.

"Did you tell Detective Collett about living at the shelter?" I asked.

"No. Mrs. Ingles would have started trying to help me, and I have to do this myself."

"Then why are you telling me?"

"Because that's where I saw the victim first," Cassidey said, finally meeting my eyes. "She came to the shelter to make a donation. Not many people do that—most just write checks and mail them in. But I heard her tell the director that she wanted to see the place before she decided whether to support it."

"I understand why you didn't want to discuss that with Denise. Did Diana see you there?"

"No, but I heard everything she said. I thought I might want to be a private investigator after watching you solve that last case, so I was... listening. But I didn't like the feeling of spying on people, so I guess I'll have to think of a different career."

"And what you overheard might help the investigation?"

"Maybe." Cassidey took a deep breath. "She told the director that she was in town because her ex-husband was here, and she needed to talk to him about something important. She didn't say who he was or give any other details."

An ex-husband. That opened up a whole new avenue of investigation—and a much more personal motive than random food tampering. I tried not to let my own experiences with divorce color my reaction, but ex-spouses definitely had the potential for murder-level animosity.

"Okay," I said carefully. "I'll need to share this information with George, and I can't keep your name out of it completely. But I can frame it to let them assume you were volunteering at the shelter rather than living there. And Cassidey? We are going to solve this case. I won't let anyone pin a murder on you."

I wasn't sure if Denise actually suspected her or was just being thorough, but either way, the detective could make Cassidey's life miserable until the real killer was found.

Cassidey studied my face for a long moment, as if running my words through some internal lie detector. Finally, she just shrugged, said "Thanks," and returned to her soup.

Outside, the rain continued to fall, washing away the last traces of what should have been a successful charity fair. But inside my warm diner, with a scared young woman finally willing to trust me with the truth, I felt the familiar stirring of determination that meant another investigation was about to begin.

## 11

C assidey had offered her help in the kitchen doing whatever Jacquie asked, so we were ready when the post-fair crowd started trickling in an hour later. We'd all agreed not to spread rumors, but collecting gossip for our own investigation was fair game. Most people didn't linger—they wanted their information fix and then they were gone—so when George and Denise walked through the door an hour before my usual closing time, we only had three customers nursing coffee at the counter.

I pointed to the booth by the front door and caught Lissa's eye, gesturing for coffee service. Cassidey, who'd been learning the closing routine in the kitchen, immediately melted out of sight.

"I won't take much of your time," George said as we settled into the booth. "Just need your statement, and then I'm afraid we'll have to close your doors."

Close the diner? The words hit me like a physical blow. "Why?" I asked, after Lissa had delivered steaming mugs of coffee and retreated to give us privacy.

"We need to find the source of contamination," Denise said with clinical detachment. "Until the medical examiner gives us more to work with, we have to minimize public health risks."

I saw George's jaw tighten slightly—whether in annoyance at his partner's bluntness or frustration with the situation, I couldn't tell.

"It's not just your place, Eliza," he said more gently. "And it's not permanent. We need to examine the preparation processes at all five establishments that had receipts in the victim's purse. Make sure nothing could have introduced peanut contamination. Let's get your statement first, though."

"You already know most of it," I said, eager to get through this so I could process the implications of being shut down. "Diana Whitfield bought one of our sample plates and asked detailed questions about allergens. I suppose peanut oil cooked into food doesn't have a distinctive smell that would warn someone. When I heard the scream, I ran over to help. Checked for a pulse, then tried to preserve the scene until you arrived. Vic brought Doc Surrey, who confirmed she was dead. You took over, and I went back to our booth."

"What about after that?" George asked, watching Denise take notes. "Any gossip, theories, or details your team remembered later?"

Did Denise tell him she suspect Cassidey had held something back? "No real rumors yet—too soon for even the Nueva Vida gossip mill to get close to anything useful. Cassidey did remember that the victim had come from the direction of Pearl's bakery booth. I think she mentioned that to Detective Collett."

"She did," Denise confirmed without looking up from

her notebook. "Though Tina Ingles did her best to interfere with my questions."

"Cassidey's only sixteen, and I think she was in shock," I said, trying to build sympathy for what I was about to reveal. "You have to remember, she's had some difficult experiences."

"She seemed fine to me," Denise said curtly. "Being in that gang probably toughened her up."

"You don't know her," I said, feeling my protective instincts flare. Denise might get results with her emotionless approach, but she needed someone like George to balance her out to actually get the whole story. "She did remember something else after we got back here."

"Or decided to tell you what she kept from us," George said knowingly. "You might as well share it."

"She overheard something relevant. Diana Whitfield's ex-husband lives somewhere in town. She came here specifically to talk to him about something."

"Where did she overhear this conversation?" Denise asked, finally looking up from her notes.

"That doesn't matter," I said firmly. "And before you tell me everything matters in a murder investigation, I'm not going to reveal that girl's private business. If you try to interrogate her about her personal situation, she'll have a lawyer present before you get her in the room."

I slid out of the booth, needing to move, to do something productive. "If we're being shut down, I should lock up and send my staff home. When will the health inspector arrive? Do you need anyone to stay?"

"As soon as we can get her here," George said. "This isn't a routine inspection, so she's dropping everything to come tonight. Who was involved in preparing the food for the fair?"

I gave him the names, then walked to the counter to usher out my last two customers before locking the front door behind them.

"Looks like we're closed down temporarily," I announced to my team. "George only needs people who were involved in prep for the fair to stick around for the inspector."

"I was here when you and Anthone did the prep work," Jacquie said, untying her apron. "Lissa can head home if she wants. I'll stay for a while, but if this inspector shows up too late, he'll have to come ask his questions at my house."

I appreciated her loyalty more than I could express. Anthone was helping her clean up the kitchen, preparing for tomorrow even though we probably wouldn't be open.

"Where's Cassidey?" I asked.

Anthone looked up from the cutting board where he was attacking a bunch of cilantro with more force than necessary. "I sent her home. She said something about being locked out if she got back too late."

The shelter, of course. They couldn't hold beds indefinitely for residents who didn't follow curfew. I didn't explain this to Anthone—it wasn't my secret to share.

"Good thing she wasn't involved in the actual food prep," I said. "Have you changed anything in the kitchen since we got back from the fair?" Part of our preparation had included carefully isolating ingredients that were on the festival's banned list.

"Everything's exactly the same as we left it," he said, bagging the cilantro and storing it in the under-counter cooler. "I figured someone would need to examine our setup."

Jacquie handed him the cleaning spray for the flat-top

grill, and they fell into their familiar closing rhythm despite the unusual circumstances.

I returned to the booth where Denise was reading a text message on her phone.

"Inspector's five minutes out," she announced.

George nodded, but before he could respond, his phone buzzed against the table. "Kramer," he answered, his tone immediately shifting to professional alertness. "Fine. Keep her there. I'm on my way."

"I guess that means I'm staying for the inspection?" Denise asked as he ended the call. "Anything I should know?"

George shook his head as he stood. "Reporter from the Nueva Vida Record making a nuisance of herself at the station. Let me know when the inspection's finished."

As he left, I settled back into the booth across from Denise, watching my team clean a kitchen that might stay closed for days. The successful charity fair felt like a lifetime ago. Now we were facing a murder investigation, a temporary shutdown, and a scared young woman who might be in more danger than any of us realized.

The evening was far from over, and I had the sinking feeling that things were about to get much more complicated.

## 12

P art of me was grateful the inspection would happen immediately. The thought of closing EB Eats for an indefinite period made my stomach clench—I could only afford to pay my staff for a few days without revenue. Denise seemed determined to ignore my questions, but I wasn't going to waste this opportunity for clarification.

"When you say 'closed,' does that mean just to customers?" I asked. There was only so much cleaning and organizing we could do during normal downtime, so a day closed meant we could do a deep clean. And maybe the inspector would give us a list of minor maintenance items to tackle—please let them be minor issues! Inspectors could be reasonable partners or nitpicking nightmares who never seemed satisfied with any solution.

"What did you have in mind?" Denise asked, keeping her gaze fixed on the street beyond the rain-streaked window. With the storm still going strong, visibility was limited to maybe half a block.

"Could we work on improvements while we're closed? After the inspection is complete, of course." I crossed my fingers under the table, hoping this would be the last time we'd have to prove that EB Eats hadn't made a fatal mistake.

"Depends on what we find," she said, then surprised me by turning away from the window with an expression that was almost sympathetic—completely different from her usual professional mask. "Look, I don't want you shut down any longer than absolutely necessary. I know how tough it is to make money in food service. I asked Delia to start with your place so we could get you reopened first if possible."

"Oh." I blinked, caught off-guard by her unexpected consideration. "I don't know what to say. Thank you."

"Don't thank me yet. I honestly don't think the contamination came from your food or any of the other vendors, but we have to follow protocol. If we skip steps and miss something, we could lose the whole case in court."

"What's your theory about how the peanut oil got into her system?" I asked, emboldened by her moment of openness.

She gave me a sharp look. "Nice try. I'm not going to discuss case details or share my gut feelings with a civilian. And you are going to stay out of police business, right?"

I was saved from having to lie outright or start an argument by a sharp knock on the front door. A tall woman with red hair stood outside in a black raincoat, juggling an umbrella and a professional-looking briefcase while trying to stay dry.

"Delia Swanson," she said as I let her in, extending a firm handshake. "You're Eliza Burton?"

I introduced myself and Denise, then gestured toward the kitchen. "Anthone's back there—he was my co-lead on the fair preparation — and Jacquie my cook. Can I get you coffee? Tea? Something to warm you up after that drive?"

"It's going to be a long night, and I'd like to get through

this as efficiently as possible," she said, shaking the rain from her coat and pulling a thick clipboard from her briefcase. "But coffee would be great if it's no trouble."

I poured her a fresh cup while she organized her paperwork, noting the methodical way she arranged forms and checklists. Everything about her movements suggested competence and experience—exactly what I hoped for in an inspector who held my business's immediate future in her hands.

"I understand this is related to the incident at the charity fair," Delia said, accepting the coffee gratefully. "I'll need to examine your entire food preparation process, focusing on allergen protocols and cross-contamination prevention. The good news is that if everything checks out here, you should be able to reopen tomorrow."

Tomorrow. The word sounded like a promise I desperately wanted to believe.

"Where would you like to start?" I asked, leading her toward the kitchen where Anthone and Jacquie were waiting with the nervous energy of students about to hear the results of a final exam.

As Delia began her inspection, I tried to push aside my growing worry about Cassidey, the investigation, and what we might discover about Diana Whitfield's ex-husband. For now, all that mattered was getting through this inspection and keeping my diner—and my team's livelihoods—intact.

But even as I answered Delia's questions about our preparation procedures, part of my mind was already planning for the investigation meeting at Kashvi's bookstore. Murder or no murder, inspection or no inspection, some promises couldn't wait.

## 13

I wanted this inspection finished as quickly as possible, for more reasons than just getting back to business. Anthone's first real test as a kitchen leader should have been straightforward—a successful charity fair where he could show off his skills and maybe give someone like Cassidey a fresh start. He'd done everything right, including taking a chance on a young woman who desperately needed one. Most restaurants were staffed with people looking for second chances, and now he understood how to manage that responsibility.

But more importantly, I was itching to join Kashvi and Jet in the back room of the bookstore where we could start our own investigation. I wasn't about to leave Cassidey at the mercy of Detective Denise Collett's interrogation style.

"We did all the prep work right here in the main kitchen," Anthone said when Delia asked him to walk her through the process. "If you'll follow me, I can show you everything step by step. We haven't started putting things back to normal yet, so you can see exactly how we organized everything."

Delia followed him into the kitchen, with me close behind and Denise bringing up the rear. Part of me hoped the inspector would enforce a "no civilians in the work area" rule, but she didn't object, and this was technically a potential crime scene inspection.

The kitchen felt cramped with four adults crammed into a space designed for a cook and maybe one helper. Delia consulted her clipboard while we arranged ourselves around the prep station.

"When do you normally clean the premises?" she asked.

Anthone glanced at me—he knew the routine, but was smart to stick to his area of expertise for the fair preparation.

"We start the dining room during the last half hour of service," I explained. "Working around any customers still finishing up—booths, tables, chairs. After the last customer leaves, we do a second pass on everything, then floors and counter stools. Jacquie usually starts kitchen cleanup while I handle the register, then we finish the kitchen together." There were plenty of exceptions to that routine depending on how busy we'd been, but I didn't want to complicate the explanation.

Jacquie stood to the side watching as the inspection proceeded. I like that she let Anthone do the talking. I guess we were both invested in his success.

Delia nodded and made a checkmark on her form. "During your fair preparation, did you work while the kitchen was serving regular customers?"

I gave Anthone an encouraging nod.

"Only when we were testing recipes and working out timing," he said. "Once we finalized the menu, I did all the actual prep after hours over several days. Then this morning I finished everything before we opened for regular service."

"I made sure he followed the rules," Jacquie said, pointing to the page of the manual on the back counter. She slipped off her apron and tossed it in the laundry with a practiced throw. "Looks like you've got everything under control. Eliza, let me know what's happening tomorrow."

Jacquie let herself out the front door and I ran to lock it behind her. Something was making her grouchy but I had no idea what. And one less person crowding the kitchen was a benefit.

"Excellent cross-contamination protocol," Delia said approvingly, as she finished reading the page. She shifted her attention. "Your usual prep work happens here?" She gestured toward the main cutting board and sink area.

This question was mine. "Yes, though we have multiple cutting boards. You'll notice the dishwasher is positioned right behind the prep station, so there's always a clean board within reach."

From there, Delia conducted what seemed like a standard health inspection. I supposed they weren't usually done when the kitchen was spotless and closed. We passed everything she could visually check, though I noticed her making written notes rather than simple checkmarks in several places.

"Walk-in cooler?" she asked.

Anthone led her to the door at the back of the kitchen, near the rear exit. While they disappeared inside, Denise tested the back door lock.

"Is this kept locked during operating hours?" she asked.

"You think someone might have snuck in and contaminated our food?" The words slipped out before I could stop them. Obviously that's exactly what she was considering.

"Just answer the question," she snapped. "I've got four

more establishments to get through tonight, and I don't know what's normal procedure for any of them."

She was going to be dealing with anxious restaurant owners for hours. I tried to keep the sympathy off my face—she wouldn't appreciate it.

"This is our service entrance for garbage disposal," I explained. "There's a small break area right outside where staff can eat or take a few minutes of fresh air. During business hours, the door stays closed but unlocked. Staff use it constantly for trash runs and breaks. The kitchen is small enough that Jacquie or I would notice if someone came through who didn't belong."

Denise nodded, then tilted her head toward the muffled conversation coming from the walk-in. "What could they be discussing in there?"

"I assume Anthone's explaining how we isolated all potential allergens in a separate cooler for the duration of the festival," I said. "Things can get hectic during service, so we wanted to eliminate any chance of accidental cross-contamination that could ruin the fair."

"You have a freezer unit?"

"We don't do much long-term storage here. There's a small freezer in the corner of the walk-in, mostly for ice cream and frozen pies."

Delia and Anthone emerged from the cooler, both looking satisfied with whatever they'd discussed.

"As far as the fair preparation is concerned, your arrangements are more than satisfactory," Delia announced, tearing off the top sheet from her clipboard and handing it to Denise. "This should work for your official records." She turned to me with a smaller piece of paper. "I'll email you a complete copy in the morning, but here are a few minor items you might want to address when you have time. Nothing urgent. You have an excellent sous chef here."

Anthone practically glowed with pride, and I didn't bother correcting her assumption. After the day he'd had—managing a major public event, dealing with a murder investigation, and surviving a health inspection—he'd earned whatever recognition came his way.

"I'll let you know when you can reopen," Denise said as we all moved toward the front door. "Don't count on it being tomorrow, though. We've expedited the lab tests, but results still take time."

Anthone locked the door behind both women and watched through the rain-streaked window until their tail-lights disappeared down the street.

"Sorry about the sous chef thing," he said. "She just assumed."

I smiled at him, feeling a surge of maternal pride. "Today, you absolutely were my sous chef. Let's finish cleaning up and get some rest."

But even as we put the kitchen to rights, my mind was already racing ahead to the meeting at Kashvi's bookstore. We had a murder to solve, and the clock was ticking.

## 14

Since we wouldn't be opening tomorrow, Anthone and I focused our cleaning efforts on the kitchen, leaving the dining room for later. We'd come in to tackle the inspector's minor recommendations and start a thorough deep clean—assuming Denise gave us permission to be here even if we couldn't reopen.

I fired off a quick text to our staff group chat, offering paid shifts for the cleaning work and making sure to include a note to Will that Cassidey could join us. An extra pair of hands would speed things along, and honestly, I wanted to keep an eye on her while the investigation was heating up.

My second text went to Kashvi and Jet: *Be there in 10, just cleaning up.*

Jet's response was immediate: *Pizza's on the way.*

I arrived at The Open Page just as Kashvi was paying the delivery driver. The warm aroma of cheese and tomato made my stomach growl—I realized I hadn't eaten anything resembling a real meal since breakfast, just leftover fair samples that barely counted as food.

In the back room, Jet stood before what I absolutely

refused to call a murder board, though that's exactly what it was. During our first case, we'd used sticky notes and string like something out of a conspiracy theorist's fever dream. After we'd solved that mystery, Kashvi had covered the wall with special whiteboard wallpaper that she normally used for inventory tracking and business planning.

Now it was wiped clean except for a single photo in the center—Diana Whitfield, probably pulled from a social media profile—staring back at us with a smile that made the whole situation feel even more tragic.

Kashvi opened the pizza box and handed me a cold beer. "We waited for you," she said, taking her first slice. "I was stuck here at the store most of the day, so I know nothing useful. Jet was managing his pottery tour, so he missed most of the drama. Let's eat first, then start mapping out what we know."

Perfect. I needed fuel and time to organize my thoughts. The day had been such a whirlwind of food service, murder, interrogations, and inspections that I could barely think straight.

"So apart from the murder," Kashvi said after we'd all taken the edge off our hunger, "how did the fair actually go?"

"The pottery tour was fantastic," Jet said, his face lighting up despite the circumstances. "I've already booked half the participants for our full festival season package."

"People absolutely loved our food," I added. "I'm definitely adding Anthone's satay to our regular specials menu —with his permission, of course. He needs to start thinking about protecting his recipe innovations if he's serious about opening his own place someday. And Cassidey worked incredibly hard. I think she was personally determined to help us win the award for highest fundraising."

"I was hoping she had some real backbone," Kashvi said approvingly. "We all want to help her, but unless she can fight for herself, we're just wasting effort. How did Anthone handle the pressure?"

We all had people we considered family who needed support. Cassidey might have the furthest to climb, but Anthone had equally big dreams that deserved nurturing.

"He's still got things to learn," I said, "but mostly because he hasn't had the opportunities yet. He's worried about being blamed for Diana's death, which is understandable, but other than that anxiety, he stayed calm and answered all the official questions professionally."

I bit into the crust of my final slice, chewing the garlicky bread slowly and savoring every burst of herb and cheese flavor. My body was finally starting to relax after the day's stress.

The pizza box was empty, and my bed was calling, but we needed to get the basics down while everything was still fresh in my memory. A little distance from the interrogations and inspection was actually helping me organize the information more clearly.

"Let's start with names," I said. "We know Diana had an ex-husband somewhere in town, but I don't know who he is."

Kashvi grabbed a marker and stood at the whiteboard. "Suspect number one?"

Jet and I both nodded, so she wrote "Ex-H?" on the wall beside Diana's photo.

"Then there are the food vendors she visited," I continued, listing the businesses from the receipts found in her purse. "Make sure you include EB Eats—we can't ignore the obvious. I think each booth had at least one helper, but I don't know all their names yet. Put the owner's name next to each business with a question mark. We'll need to interview all of them."

"Was anyone acting particularly suspicious today?" Jet asked. "Either too interested in what was happening, or suspiciously disinterested?"

I'd been too focused on managing our booth and protecting Cassidey to do much people-watching. "I'll think about it tonight and see what comes back to me. But Alistair was definitely at his dramatic worst, making accusations without any evidence whatsoever."

Kashvi giggled as she added his name to the persons of interest list. "I wish I could let him see this board. Maybe it would teach him to keep his wild theories to himself."

"More likely it would just crank up his paranoia to eleven," Jet said with a grin. "Actually, there was someone who seemed off today, though not about the murder. The guy who won the raffle grand prize didn't seem excited at all. I know a thousand dollars isn't life-changing money, but it's still a nice windfall. His reaction was just... weird."

"Do you know his name?" Kashvi asked, marker poised. "It might be nothing, but like you said, it was a thousand dollars. Most people would at least smile."

"I've seen him around town, but I don't know who he is. I'm sure one of our information sources will be able to identify him."

Another question mark went up on the wall. We'd cross them off as we learned more, but it was disheartening to see how little we actually knew. Nothing seemed connected yet.

"I'm beat," I announced, feeling the full weight of the day settling into my bones. "What's our first move tomorrow? I can leave the deep cleaning to the others—it'll be good experience for Anthone to manage a project, and Cassidey could use the paid work."

"Interview the other food vendors," Jet said. "I can help in the afternoon, but I've got a morning tour booked."

"I'm out too," Kashvi said apologetically. "Big inventory delivery coming in, and Mallory can't handle both the store customers and the receiving process."

I shouldn't tackle the interviews alone, but I was too tired to figure out an alternative right now. "I'll work something out. Right now I just need to get home, apologize to Macchiato for abandoning her all day, clean up whatever mess she's left to express her displeasure, and collapse into bed."

"Don't go interviewing people by yourself," Jet said, his tone suddenly serious. "If one of those vendors is our killer, you could be putting yourself in danger. It can wait until afternoon."

I was too exhausted to argue, but I knew myself well enough to recognize that I wouldn't be sitting around waiting for backup when there were answers to be found.

Some things were worth the risk.

## 15

I woke to Macchiato sitting on my chest, fixing me with the laser-focused stare of a cat who'd been awake for hours contemplating her human's breakfast negligence. Morning light filtered through my bedroom window with a gentleness that yesterday's harsh sun had lacked, and I could hear birds chattering outside instead of the ominous silence that usually preceded another scorching day.

"Good morning to you too, your majesty," I murmured, scratching behind her ears until she purred and gracefully dismounted to lead me toward her empty food bowl.

My phone showed three messages. Jacquie had sent a photo of herself and Will already at the diner, both giving enthusiastic thumbs up while brandishing cleaning supplies. Anthone had texted that Cassidey would arrive at nine and asked if I wanted him to wait for me before starting the deep clean. The third message was from Kashvi: *Call when you're ready to investigate. I found something.*

After appeasing Macchiato with her breakfast and brewing myself a proper cup of coffee, I called Anthone.

"We're making excellent progress," he said, and I could

hear genuine satisfaction in his voice. "Jacquie has Will scrubbing surfaces that probably haven't seen this much attention since it first opened. I think she's enjoying having someone new to boss around who isn't me."

I laughed, imagining Will's expression under Jacquie's enthusiastic supervision. "How's Cassidey doing?"

"She showed up at eight-thirty, which tells you something about the shelter's morning routine. Yeah she told my about her situation. Don't worry—I fed her first thing. She's meticulous with detail work, and she actually asks questions when she doesn't understand something instead of pretending she knows."

That sounded promising for someone trying to build legitimate work experience. "I need to make a few stops this morning. Can you handle things without me for a while?"

"Absolutely. Though if you're planning to talk to the other food vendors, maybe I should come along? We're all in the same boat right now—might be better to approach this as mutual support rather than interrogation."

Smart thinking. Having Anthone there would make the conversations feel more collaborative and less suspicious. "Good idea. Can you break away around ten?"

"Make it ten-thirty. I want to make sure Cassidey's comfortable with her tasks before I leave her with Jacquie and Will's enthusiasm."

After we hung up, I called Kashvi.

"I did some digging last night," she said without preamble. "Diana Whitfield, fifty-two, divorced last year from David Sterling in Santa Fe. Clean record, worked in marketing before the divorce settlement. Here's the interesting part—she's been staying at the Turquoise Inn for the past week."

"A whole week? That's a long time for a casual tourist visit."

"Exactly what I thought. And here's the kicker—the divorce was apparently brutal. There's a public record of a restraining order she filed against him, though she dropped it about a month later."

I felt that familiar spark of connections forming. "So she came to Nueva Vida specifically to confront her ex-husband, who must live here somewhere."

"That's my theory. Want to meet at the bookstore after you finish with the vendors? I'm going to keep digging into David Sterling's background."

AN HOUR LATER, Anthone and I approached Frontier Burgers, first stop on our informal vendor support tour. The restaurant looked weary in the morning light—paint peeling around window frames, a hand-lettered sign that had seen better years. But the aroma that greeted us was exactly right: beef on the grill, caramelized onions, that distinctive smell of a place that understood how to make an honest burger.

"We're closed," called a voice from behind the cooking area. A man emerged, wiping his hands on a towel—probably mid-fifties, with the solid build of someone who'd spent years in commercial kitchens. "Oh, you're from EB Eats. Bernie Castro." He extended his hand. "Heard you got the same royal treatment from the health inspector."

"Eliza, and this is Anthone," I said, returning his handshake. "We thought maybe we should compare notes. This whole situation has everyone pretty shaken."

Bernie gestured toward a corner booth. "Coffee? About the only thing I'm allowed to serve right now. I'm testing a few new versions of my patties but... we'll you know. I can't let you try them."

We accepted his offer, and Bernie returned with three cups of surprisingly excellent coffee.

"Been thinking about this all night," he said, settling across from us. "The thing about peanut oil—that's not something you accidentally introduce into food. Someone had to add it deliberately."

"You mean after she'd already bought the food?" Anthone asked.

"Has to be," Bernie said firmly. "We all received those banned ingredient lists months ago. And peanut oil has a distinctive smell when you're cooking with it. Not overpowering, but anyone who knows food would notice it immediately."

"So someone followed her around the fairgrounds?" The logistics seemed complicated for a random attack.

Bernie stirred sugar into his coffee thoughtfully. "Or they knew she'd be there. Knew about her allergy. That would make it premeditated, wouldn't it?"

We sat with that uncomfortable reality for a moment.

"Do you know anything about Diana Whitfield personally?" I asked.

"Nothing really. Never saw her before yesterday, as far as I can remember. Though..." He paused, frowning. "There was something when she came to my booth. She seemed vaguely familiar, but I couldn't place her. You know how it is —maybe she resembled someone else."

"The police seem convinced one of us made a preparation error," Anthone said. "But you're absolutely right about the oil. I would have detected it in my cooking process."

"Of course you would." Bernie's voice carried the automatic solidarity of one professional cook supporting another. "That Detective Collett, though—she's determined to prove one of us is lying. Asked me three separate times if I was certain about my ingredients."

"She's taking the same approach with everyone," I said. "What's your read on the other vendors?"

Bernie's expression darkened slightly. "Well, there's one person who's been making noise about all of us for months. Alistair McKay has been telling anyone who'll listen that the competition has gotten too intense, that some of us shouldn't be permitted at community events."

"He made similar comments to us," Anthone said. "Seems convinced we're all conspiring to destroy his business."

"The man's been struggling for years," Bernie said. "But instead of improving his offerings, he'd rather undermine everyone else's reputation. I've heard him criticize every vendor here at various times."

The entrance bell chimed, and Pearl Sargent from Pane de Vida bakery walked in, looking as exhausted as I felt.

"Jacquie said I might find you here," she said to me. "Mind if I join this impromptu support group?"

"The more voices, the better," Bernie said, sliding over to make room.

Pearl accepted coffee and settled in with a weary sigh. "Spent half the night wondering if I'd somehow contaminated my flour supplies with peanut powder. But I checked everything twice yesterday morning, same as always."

"We were just discussing how the oil must have been added after the food was prepared," I said.

"That makes the most sense," Pearl agreed. "Poor woman. And that young lady helping you—Cassidey? I heard Detective Collett has been particularly aggressive with her questioning."

"Because she's an easy target," Anthone said, his protective instincts evident. "She only handled money and customer service. Never touched any food preparation."

"Still," Bernie said carefully, "she does have those gang associations. People might naturally wonder..."

"People can wonder all they want," I said firmly. "Cassidey worked harder than anyone yesterday, and she was nothing but professional and helpful. Besides, what possible motive would she have for hurting a complete stranger?"

Pearl nodded approvingly. "That's exactly what I told my Harold when he started speculating. The girl's trying to build a legitimate life for herself. We should be supporting that effort, not tearing her down with gossip."

"Has anyone heard when we might be allowed to reopen?" Bernie asked.

"Hopefully tomorrow," I said. "Depends on how quickly the lab processes the test results."

"Better be soon," Pearl said. "I have three dozen custom cupcakes due for the Martinez anniversary celebration this weekend. If I have to close my kitchen for much longer, I'll need to make alternative arrangements."

Bernie stood to refill our cups. "You know, Anthone," he said while pouring, "when this situation resolves, I might have a business proposition for you. Been considering expanding my catering operation, maybe adding sophisticated appetizers like those you served yesterday. Could use someone with your culinary skills."

Anthone's eyes brightened with interest. "Catering work?"

"Wedding receptions, corporate events, that sort of thing. Better pay than standard diner work, and you'd have creative freedom with menu development. Think it over."

I felt a complex mix of emotions—pride in Anthone's

growing professional reputation, and a pang of sadness at the prospect of losing him. But that was the essential purpose of mentoring, wasn't it? Helping someone discover their own path forward.

"I definitely will," Anthone said. "Thank you for considering me."

The door chimed again, admitting Miguel from Los Amigos. Within fifteen minutes, we had an impromptu gathering of all the affected vendors except Alistair, sharing coffee and mutual frustrations.

"The worst aspect," said Lisa from Tropical Smoothies, "is feeling like we're all under constant suspicion. I keep second-guessing every single thing I did yesterday."

"That's exactly what we shouldn't do," Miguel said firmly. "We followed proper protocols. We prepared quality food. Someone else was responsible for this tragedy."

"The question is who," Pearl said quietly.

We all looked at each other, the weight of that question settling over our small group like storm clouds.

"Well," I said finally, "I suppose we'll discover the answer soon enough."

## 16

An hour later, Anthone and I walked into The Open Page to see Kashvi surrounded by printouts, her laptop open, and several notebooks scattered across her usual table in the back of the store. She looked up as we approached, her expression a mix of excitement and concern.

"Perfect timing," she said, gesturing for us to sit. "I've been digging deeper into Diana Whitfield's background, and there's definitely more to this story. Close the door, we don't want Mallory overhearing us. She'd want in and I'm not ready to put anyone at risk."

I accepted the coffee she'd already prepared for us— Kashvi always thought ahead when it came to caffeine—and settled into the familiar chair. The bookstore's quiet atmosphere was a welcome change from the morning's conversations with the other vendors.

"What did you find?" Anthone asked, leaning forward with interest.

Kashvi shuffled through her papers until she found what

she was looking for. "So Diana Whitfield, divorced from David Sterling last year. The divorce was nasty—really nasty. There are court records of her filing a restraining order against him, claiming he'd threatened her when she asked for the divorce."

"You mentioned she dropped the restraining order," I said, thinking back to my own divorce, unpleasant, but not even close to nasty.

"She did, but get this—the divorce settlement was huge. She got almost everything. Their house in Santa Fe, most of their investment portfolio, and apparently he had to pay significant alimony. From what I can piece together from public records, she walked away with several million dollars."

Anthone whistled low. "That's serious money. Definitely enough to hold a grudge over. Is it normal? I thought divorce meant a 50/50 split."

"I think she might have had some dirt on him. He probably wanted her to keep quiet and it cost him everything. And, it gets more interesting," Kashvi continued, pulling up something on her laptop. "David Sterling moved to Nueva Vida about six months ago. He bought a small place on Cottonwood Street—paid cash, but nothing like the house I found that he lost in the divorce."

"So he's definitely in town," I said. "Have you seen him around? Do we know what he looks like?"

Kashvi turned her laptop toward us, showing a social media profile. "This is from before the divorce, but it's the most recent photo I could find. I'll print it for the wall later."

The man in the picture was probably in his mid-fifties, with graying hair and the kind of lean build that suggested he stayed active. He had an easy smile in the photo, but there was something about his eyes that seemed guarded.

He looked vaguely familiar, though I couldn't place where I might have seen him.

"He looks like he could be anyone," Anthone observed. "The kind of guy who'd blend into a crowd at the fair."

"Exactly what I was thinking," Kashvi said. "And remember, Diana had been staying at the Turquoise Inn for a week. That's not tourist behavior. She was here for a specific purpose."

"To confront him about something," I said, thinking through the timeline. "But what? The divorce was finalized months ago."

"Maybe there was something unresolved," Anthone suggested. "Or maybe she discovered something new about their finances."

Kashvi made a note in her notebook. "I tried to find more recent information about David Sterling, but he's kept a very low profile since moving here. No social media activity, no local business registrations. It's like he's trying to disappear."

"Or just trying to start over," I said, though I wasn't entirely convinced. "What about employment? Is he working anywhere in town?"

"That's what I want to find out next. I thought maybe we could drive by his address, see if he's home or if there are any clues about what he's been doing."

The door chime announced a customer, and Kashvi excused herself to help an elderly man looking for a specific history book. While she was gone, Anthone and I studied the information she'd gathered. None of it was organized enough to put on the murder board, but still important to finding a real suspect.

"This feels different from last time," Anthone said

quietly. "More personal, somehow. Or maybe it's because I wasn't involved in your last investigation."

He was right. Our previous case had felt like solving a puzzle, but this one had an undercurrent of real pain—a marriage that had ended badly, a woman who'd died alone at what should have been a community celebration. I wasn't feeling great about Anthone seeing all this, but maybe it was good to share our investigation, get a new perspective.

"Diana came here to tell him something," I said, thinking out loud. "Something important enough that she couldn't just call or send a letter."

"And someone killed her before she could deliver the message," Anthone added. "Or because of it."

Kashvi returned, looking pleased. "Found his book and discovered he's actually Martha Hendricks' cousin. She might know something about David Sterling."

"Martha from the post office?" I asked. Martha knew everyone in Nueva Vida and most of their business.

"The very same. I was thinking we could stop by there after we check out Sterling's house. She'd be a goldmine of information, and she actually likes sharing what she knows —makes her feel important."

"Good thinking," I said. "What about Jet? Is he free to join us?"

"His tour runs until three, but he said he'd meet us at David Sterling's house around four if we want backup."

I checked my watch. It was just past noon. "That gives us time to scout the location and talk to Martha. Should we call George and let him know what we've found?"

Kashvi and Anthone exchanged glances. "You know he's going to tell us to stay out of it," Kashvi said.

"And he'd be right," I admitted. "But if David Sterling is

our killer, we can't just sit around waiting for the police to figure it out. Not with Cassidey still on their suspect list."

"Plus," Anthone added, "we're not exactly interfering with their investigation. We're just... gathering information."

I smiled at his careful phrasing—something we'd used to convince ourselves. "Exactly. We're being helpful citizens."

## 17

Twenty minutes later, we were in my car, driving slowly down Cottonwood Street while Kashvi consulted the address she'd found. The neighborhood was modest but well-maintained, with small adobe houses and yards full of desert landscaping.

"There," she said, pointing to a small house with brown trim and a neatly kept yard. "That's 412."

I parked across the street, and we sat for a moment studying the house. It looked quiet—no car in the driveway, no signs of activity. The front curtains were drawn, making it impossible to see inside.

"Doesn't look like anyone's at home," Anthone observed.

"He could be at work," I said. "Or deliberately avoiding visitors."

As we watched, a neighbor emerged from the house next door—an elderly woman in a sun hat, carrying a watering can. She moved slowly among the plants in her front yard, but I noticed she kept glancing toward David Sterling's house.

"She might know something," Kashvi said, following my gaze. "And she kind of looks like she's worried about him."

"Worth a try," I agreed, crossing my fingers. Old ladies noticed a lot, but not all of them were willing to talk. "Let's go introduce ourselves."

We approached the woman with friendly smiles. She looked up as we neared her fence, her expression curious but cautious.

"Beautiful garden," I said genuinely. Her yard was full of desert plants that looked healthy despite the recent heat.

"Thank you," she said, warming slightly. "I'm Ruth Morrison. I don't think we've met."

"I'm Eliza Burton—I own EB Eats, the diner downtown. This is Kashvi and Anthone."

Recognition flickered in her eyes. "Oh, you're the one who had the trouble at the fair yesterday. Terrible business, that poor woman dying."

"It's been very upsetting," I agreed. "We're just trying to understand what happened. I hope you don't mind me asking, but do you know your neighbor? David Sterling?"

Ruth's expression shifted, becoming more guarded. "I know him to say hello. Keeps to himself mostly. Why do you ask?"

"We heard he might have known the woman who died," Kashvi said carefully. "We're just trying to piece together what happened."

Ruth set down her watering can and looked directly at us. "Are you working with the police?" there was something more than normal caution in her tone.

"Informally," I said, which wasn't exactly a lie. "We want to make sure they have all the information they need."

She considered this for a moment, then glanced toward David Sterling's house. "He's been acting strange lately.

More so than usual, I mean. David's always been quiet, but this past week he's seemed... nervous. Jumpy."

"This past week specifically?" Anthone asked.

"Yes. Called my son Tom to look at his truck, nothing wrong apparently." She threw another look at the house next door. "And he's had a visitor—a woman. I saw her coming and going several times. Blond, nicely dressed. Drove a rental car."

My pulse quickened. Was this our victim? "Did you see her recently? Like yesterday?"

"Well, that's the odd thing," Ruth said, lowering her voice as if sharing a secret. "I saw her car here yesterday morning, early. But when I looked again after lunch, it was gone, and David's truck wasn't in the driveway either. Haven't seen either of them since."

Kashvi and I exchanged looks. Diana had been at David Sterling's house the morning of the fair, and now both of them were missing.

"Do you know where David works?" I asked.

"That's another strange thing," Ruth said. "Far as I can tell, he doesn't work anywhere regular. But he's scraping by somehow—paid cash for the house, but it's a small place, and his truck's getting pretty worn. Makes me wonder what he's living on."

"Maybe he had some savings?" Kashvi suggested.

Ruth shook her head. "From what I gathered when he moved in, his ex-wife cleaned him out in the divorce. Left him with just enough to buy this little place and start over. He's bitter about it—I've heard him muttering over it when he works in his yard."

She had a point. If David Sterling had lost most of his assets in the divorce, that would explain both his modest living situation and his potential resentment toward Diana. But why would she visit him?

"Mrs. Morrison," I said carefully, "if you see David come back, would you mind giving me a call? Here's my number." I handed her one of the diner's business cards. "We're just concerned about making sure everyone's safe."

She tucked the card into her gardening apron. "I'll keep an eye out. And you be careful, dear. If that man had something to do with what happened at the fair, you don't want to be poking around too much."

## 18

Martha Hendricks was exactly where we expected to find her—behind the post office counter, sorting mail with methodical precision—exactly what I expected of a woman who'd been doing the job for decades. She looked up as we entered, her face brightening with at the chance to gather or give out gossip. Martha thrived on being the center of Nueva Vida's information network.

"Well, if it isn't our local Nancy Drew and the Hardy Boys," she said with a grin that made her look ten years younger. "I heard you folks were making the rounds, asking questions about that poor woman who died at the fair."

I had to smile. Martha's enthusiasm for drama rivaled that of any soap opera fan, and she wore her role as town information broker like a badge of honor. When she came into the diner she ordered the same thing every time: a tuna fish sandwich and coke.

"Word travels fast," I said, approaching the counter trying to think of the best way to open the subject without setting off a two hour rendition of family drama.

"Honey, in a town this size, news travels faster than Tina Ingles chasing down a new side gig," Martha replied, setting aside her mail sorting. "What can I help you with? And don't pretend this is a social visit—I can see that investigative gleam in your eyes."

Kashvi stepped forward with her notebook ready, looking every inch the determined researcher. "We heard you might know David Sterling. He lives on Cottonwood Street?"

Martha's expression immediately shifted from amused to serious, like an actor switching roles mid-scene. "David Sterling. Yes, I know him. What do you want to know?"

Interesting reaction. Was she trying to protect him or boost the tension? "We're trying to understand his connection to Diana Whitfield," I said. "We think they might have known each other."

"Oh, they knew each other all right," Martha said, leaning forward conspiratorially. Her voice dropped to what she probably thought was a whisper but could likely be heard in the next county. "They were married. Divorced about a year ago, from what I gather. Messier than Alistair's attempt at holiday decorating."

I bit back a smile at the mental image of Alistair wrestling with Christmas lights. "How do you know all this?"

Martha tapped the side of her nose with pride of knowing everyone's business. "David's been getting mail forwarded here from Santa Fe. Legal documents, mostly. And Diana Whitfield has been sending him registered letters for months. Always had to sign for them himself— never let anyone else take delivery. Made him more nervous than a cat in a dog park every time one arrived."

"Registered letters?" Kashvi made a note. "That sounds official."

"Legal stuff, I'd guess. Divorce papers, maybe financial documents. The man always looked like he was expecting bad news when he had to sign for them." Martha paused, studying our faces with the intensity of someone reading auras. "You think he had something to do with her death?"

The question hung in the air with the weight of small-town speculation. I could practically see Martha's mental wheels turning, already composing the story she'd share with her next customer. I didn't like being the object of gossip, but I couldn't do anything about the rumor mill. And here I was taking advantage of it, so I guess it was tit-for-tat.

"We're just trying to understand the situation," I said carefully. "Have you seen David recently?"

"Not since yesterday morning. He came in early, maybe around seven-thirty, looking more agitated than usual. Asked if he had any mail, which was odd because he knows I don't usually sort the mail until after nine. Man was jumpier than popcorn in a hot pan."

"Did he seem upset about something specific?" Kashvi asked.

"Well, that's the interesting part," Martha said, clearly enjoying having a captive audience for her tale. "He asked me if anyone had been looking for him. Wanted to know if strangers had been inquiring about his address or personal information. Made me wonder if he was expecting trouble."

My pulse quickened. Suspicious behavior was the best clue we had so far. "What did you tell him?"

"The truth—that no one had asked about him recently. But he seemed relieved, like he'd been holding his breath waiting for bad news."

I found myself liking Martha despite her obvious love of

gossip—or maybe because of it. At least she was honest about sharing information rather than pretending to be discreet while spreading stories anyway. That way everyone knew where to come for dirt—information I mean—and everyone knew she'd share what she knew.

"Martha," I said, "this might be important. Do you know if David has any family in town? Anyone he might be close to?"

She considered this carefully, her expression taking on the thoughtful look as she accessed her vast mental database. "He's mentioned a son a few times. Jake something-or-other. Different last name, though—I think the boy took his mother's name when his parents split up years ago. David seemed pretty bitter about that whole situation."

"There aren't too many men with that name. If they are both new to town, that would be Jake Webb?" Kashvi asked, her pen poised.

"That sounds right. I do know him, odd I didn't make the connection. Nice young man, actually. Works at the hardware store part-time, I think. Comes in here occasionally to mail packages to his grandmother or some such. Always polite, always says please and thank you. Reminds me of my own grandson, except he actually visits."

I felt a spark of recognition. "Tall kid, dark hair? Maybe early twenties?"

"That's him. You know Jake?" Martha said with a glance over my shoulder to the street. Like she was hinting the conversation was coming to an end.

"I think I've seen him around town," I said, though I couldn't quite place where. The feeling nagged at me like trying to remember the name of a song you can hum but can't identify. "Or maybe in the store?"

"Do you know if he and his father get along?" Anthone asked.

Martha laughed, but there wasn't much humor in it. "From what I can tell, they get along about as well as oil and water. Jake comes in here sometimes, and if David happens to be around, they avoid each other like they're carrying contagious diseases. Family drama—you know how it is."

I did know, unfortunately. My own divorce had left enough emotional wreckage that I could sympathize with complicated family dynamics, even if they didn't extend to murder.

"Has Jake been in recently?" Anthone asked.

She scratched her temple as if trying to bring up a memory. "He was here yesterday afternoon, maybe around two o'clock. Seemed anxious about something—kept checking his phone and looking around like he was expecting someone. Asked if his father had been in, and when I said yes, he looked relieved. Struck me as odd at the time."

I exchanged glances with Kashvi. The timing was interesting—Jake checking on his father's whereabouts after Diana's death had been discovered.

"Martha," I said, "if either David or Jake comes in again, would you mind giving me a call?" I handed her another business card. "We're just trying to help the police understand what happened. Maybe you should pass this on to George or his partner."

"Of course, dear. This whole situation has everyone on edge. Makes you wonder who you can trust." She tucked the card into her cash drawer with the care of someone filing important documents. "But you be careful. If David Sterling is involved in that woman's death, he might not appreciate people asking questions about him."

## 19

As we left the post office, I noticed a young man approaching from across the street. Tall, dark-haired, early twenties—exactly matching Martha's description of Jake Webb. He was walking directly toward the post office, but when he saw us emerging from the building, he stopped abruptly, like a deer caught in headlights.

"That him?" Kashvi whispered. "What are the odds?"

"I think so," I murmured back, studying his face. There was something familiar about him, but I still couldn't place it. I guess it didn't matter, we knew his name and relationship to the victim.

Jake stood there for a moment, clearly uncertain whether to continue toward the post office or beat a hasty retreat. Finally, he seemed to make a decision and approached us with what looked like forced casualness— the kind of deliberate nonchalance that immediately made you suspicious.

"Excuse me," he said, his voice pleasant but with an underlying tension that reminded me of guitar strings wound too tight. "Aren't you the folks from the diner? The ones who had the booth at the fair yesterday?"

"That's right," I said, extending my hand with automatic friendliness that came with working in the restaurant business. "I'm Eliza Burton. This is Kashvi and Anthone."

"Jake Webb," he said, shaking hands with each of us. His grip was firm, but I noticed his palms were slightly damp. Nervous, or just warm from the afternoon heat? "I'm really sorry about what happened yesterday. Must have been terrible for everyone involved."

"It was pretty shocking," I agreed, studying his face more carefully. He had the kind of open, pleasant features that would make him popular with customers, but there was something about his eyes that didn't quite match his concerned expression. Like someone tasting something they hated but had to be polite about it.

"I heard the police are investigating all the food vendors," he continued, shifting his weight from foot to foot in a way that reminded me of Cassidey when she was nervous. "That must be stressful, having your business shut down while they figure things out."

"We're hoping to reopen soon," Anthone said with more optimism than I felt. "Once they complete their tests."

"Good, good," Jake said, his tone carrying the forced enthusiasm of someone making small talk at a funeral. "The diner's important to the community. I hope this whole thing gets resolved quickly."

I found myself wondering about his story. Was he genuinely concerned about local businesses, or was there another reason he was so interested in our situation?

"Did you know the woman who died?" Kashvi asked suddenly, her investigative instincts cutting straight to the heart of the matter. "Diana Whitfield?"

Jake's expression flickered for just a moment—so briefly I almost missed it. It was like watching someone stumble and quickly regain their balance. "No, I don't think so. The name doesn't sound familiar. Was she from around here?"

The words came too easily, too quickly to be the truth. In my experience, when people didn't know someone, they usually took a moment to think about it, maybe searched their memory. Jake's immediate denial felt rehearsed. It's possible he didn't know his dad's ex-wife, but highly improbable.

"She was visiting," I said, watching his reaction carefully. "We heard she might have had family connections in town."

"Oh," Jake said, and now he definitely looked uncomfortable, like he'd walked into the wrong conversation. "Well, I hope the police find out what happened. I should probably get going—I was just stopping by the post office to see if there's news from my grandmother."

The mention of his grandmother felt like truth, which made his lie about Diana even more obvious by contrast.

"Of course," I said with the same pleasant tone I used for customers who complained about their food after eating most of it. "Nice meeting you, Jake."

We watched him walk into the post office, and I noticed he kept glancing back at us through the window like he was expecting us to watch him, or to see if he was being followed.

"He's lying," Kashvi said quietly as we walked away.

"About what?" Anthone asked.

"About not knowing Diana Whitfield. Did you see his face when I mentioned her name? He definitely recognized it." Kashvi's voice carried conviction as if we'd solved so many crimes no one could fool us.

I nodded, remembering that brief flicker of something—

fear? guilt? recognition?—that had crossed his features. "And he seemed awfully interested in the police investigation for someone who's just a concerned community member."

"Plus," Anthone added with the logical thinking that would serve him well as a restaurant owner, "if his father is David Sterling and his last name is Webb, that means he took his mother's name. Not exactly a sign of a happy relationship."

We reached my car and stood there for a moment, processing what we'd learned. The afternoon sun was getting lower, casting longer shadows that made everything look more dramatic than it probably was.

"So Jake Webb is David Sterling's son," I said, thinking through the implications. "And despite Martha's impression that they don't get along, Jake was checking on his father's whereabouts yesterday afternoon."

"Maybe they're not as estranged as they want people to believe," Kashvi suggested, her notebook already filling with theories.

"Or maybe Jake was worried about what his father might have done," Anthone said. "Hey, I know where I've seen him before. He was the guy who won the first prize in the raffle."

"The one you said didn't seem happy about it?" I asked. There was too much information coming at me and no time to process it into useful clues.

"Yep," Anthone said with a shrug. "You know, I'm glad I can go back to working at the diner and don't have to keep investigating. I'm only here to help you keep Cassidey safe."

I looked back toward the post office, where I could see Jake talking animatedly with Martha through the window. His body language was more relaxed now, which suggested he was more comfortable with her than he'd been with us.

"Either way," I said, "I think Jake Webb just became a person of interest in our investigation."

"Should we follow him when he leaves?" Kashvi asked, her eyes bright with the thrill of the chase.

I considered it, but decided against it. "Not yet. Let's see what else we can find out about the family dynamics first. And I want to talk to Jet when he gets back from his tour. He might have seen something at the fair that we missed."

As we drove away, I couldn't shake the feeling that our conversation with Jake Webb had revealed more than he'd intended. He lied about almost everything, but he might not know we know that. The question was whether he was trying to protect his father or himself. Or maybe both.

But more importantly, I found myself thinking about the contrast between him and Cassidey. Yesterday, she'd been as unsure of herself as he played at being. By afternoon she was confident. And this morning, working legitimate jobs, being trusted with responsibility, earning honest money—it was transforming her in ways that reminded me why I'd gotten into the restaurant business in the first place. Sometimes feeding people was about more than just food.

I made a mental note to talk to her about more hours at the diner. The budget would be tight, but if I couldn't scrimp a little in a good cause, what was the point?

If we could solve this murder case and get back to normal operations, maybe we could offer Cassidey the stability she needed to completely leave her old life behind. And I had a few ideas about getting her out of that shelter.

After all, everyone deserved a second chance—or in Cassidey's case, maybe a first real chance at a legitimate future.

## 20

B y the time we returned to EB Eats, the afternoon cleaning crew had transformed the place. The dining room gleamed, every surface polished and sanitized. Through the kitchen pass-through, I could see Cassidey methodically organizing supplies while Will scrubbed the baseboards with the intensity of someone who'd been given very specific instructions by Jacquie.

"How's it going?" I called out as we entered. I missed the tantalizing aroma of grilled and fried food, but food service didn't just mean cooking, and the scent of cleaning was comforting too.

Cassidey looked up with a smile that transformed her entire face. "Really good! Jacquie's teaching me how to do inventory, and Anthone said maybe I could help with prep work once we reopen."

"That's wonderful," I said, meaning it. "You're doing great work."

Jacquie emerged from the kitchen, wiping her hands on a towel. "This girl's got natural organizational skills," she announced. "And she asks smart questions. You should consider keeping her on permanent. Teach her some life skills."

I saw Cassidey's eyes light up with excitement, quickly followed by the caution I knew she'd learned about not expecting good things to last.

"Let's see how everything goes," I said gently. "But you're definitely proving yourself."

My phone buzzed with a text from Jet: *Tour finished early. Meet at bookstore? Have some info to share.*

"We should head back," I told Kashvi and Anthone. "Jet's ready to compare notes."

"Can I come with you?" Cassidey asked suddenly, then immediately looked embarrassed. "I mean, if it's about the case. I might know something useful."

I hesitated. Getting a sixteen-year-old more involved in a murder investigation went against every responsible instinct I had. But she was already involved, whether I liked it or not, and keeping her informed might be better than leaving her to worry.

"It's just discussion," I said finally. "No field work, no confronting anyone. Just sharing information."

"I promise," she said eagerly.

Five minutes later, we were gathered in Kashvi's back room again—a little crowded but eager to see all the information laid out. Jet had taped a hand-drawn map of the fairgrounds on the wall, with various locations marked in different colored pens. If our team got bigger, we'd need to relocate. Not that we'd make a habit of investigating!

"I've been thinking about the timeline," he said without preamble. "And there are some interesting patterns."

He pointed to various spots on his map. "I tracked my tour group's movements throughout the day, and we passed the picnic area several times. I can account for when Diana was at different food booths based on when my people saw her."

"This is impressive," Anthone said, studying the detailed map.

"What did you notice?" I asked.

Jet opened his notebook. "Well, according to my notes and my tour group's observations, Diana visited the food booths in this order." He traced a path with his finger. "Los Amigos around eleven-thirty, your booth around noon, Pan de Vida bakery about twelve-fifteen, Tropical Smoothies at twelve-thirty, and Frontier Burgers last, maybe around twelve-forty-five."

Cassidey shifted in her chair. I gave her a nod to say what was on her mind. "I thought she was at the bakery first. I remember sugar on her lips as I sold her one of our samples."

Jet put a question mark beside the order on the wall. "It might be nothing, maybe she went there twice?"

"The original timeline matches the timestamps on the receipts," Kashvi said, consulting her notes. "My best romance reader, Betty, send them to me last night."

"Here's the interesting part," Jet continued. "One of my tour participants—Mrs. Chen from Phoenix—noticed Diana at the picnic tables around one o'clock. She was sitting alone, eating, and seemed to be waiting for someone."

"Waiting for someone?" I leaned forward. "Did Mrs. Chen see who?"

"That's where it gets tricky. Mrs. Chen said a man approached Diana's table around one-fifteen. They talked for maybe ten minutes, and it looked like a tense conversation. Then the man left, and Diana remained at the table."

"Can she describe the man?" Kashvi asked, pen ready.

"Average height, wearing a baseball cap and sunglasses. Mrs. Chen said she couldn't see his face clearly, but their body language suggested they knew each other."

"That could be David Sterling," I said.

"Or Jake Webb," Anthone added. "He's not that tall and sitting might make him seem average, especially from from a distance."

Cassidey, who had been listening quietly, suddenly spoke up. "What time did the screaming start?"

Jet checked his notes. "According to my log, around two-fifteen. Why?"

"Because I saw someone running away from the picnic area right after," she said. "I was near the pottery booth, trying to get people to come to our station, when I heard the scream. I looked toward the sound, and I saw someone moving fast through the crowd, heading toward the parking area." She looked down at her hands when she stopped talking like she expected to be reprimanded.

"Male or female?" I asked. I couldn't fix what made her so skittish, but I could treat her like she was adding valuable information—mostly because she was.

"Male, I think. But I only caught a glimpse. He was wearing dark clothes and moving really quickly, like he was trying to get away without running so fast that people would notice."

"Did you tell Detective Collett about this?" Kashvi asked.

Cassidey shook her head. "She didn't ask about what I saw after the scream. She was more focused on what happened at our booth. So I guess I didn't think of it. I guess things get forgotten? And talking about all the details helps me remember?"

I made a mental note to make sure George knew about

this observation. "Can you recall anything else about the person you saw?"

Cassidey closed her eyes, concentrating. "He was maybe average height, but it was hard to tell because he was kind of hunched over and everyone was moving around so I couldn't compare. And..." She paused, frowning. "I think he was carrying something. Like a small bag or container."

"A container?" Jet asked. "What kind?"

She gave a little shrug and then closed her eyes again. "Maybe like a water bottle? Or one of those small plastic containers people use for snacks. It was hard to see clearly. I didn't know it would be important."

The room went quiet as we processed this information. Someone leaving the scene quickly, carrying a container that could have held peanut oil.

"We need to tell George about this," I said. I didn't enjoy holding back information, even though we did it all the time.

"But first," Kashvi said, standing with her notebook. "Let's figure out what we know for sure."

She moved to the whiteboard and started organizing our information:

Timeline:

11:30 AM - Diana at Los Amigos

12:00 PM - Diana at EB Eats

12:15 PM - Diana at Pan de Vida

12:30 PM - Diana at Tropical Smoothies

12:45 PM - Diana at Frontier Burgers

1:00 PM - Diana at picnic table, alone

1:15 PM - Unknown man talks to Diana (10 minutes)

2:15 PM - Diana found dead

2:15 PM - Man seen leaving area quickly with container

. . .

KEY PLAYERS:

David Sterling (ex-husband, missing since yesterday)

Jake Webb (son with different last name, lied about knowing Diana—his stepmother)

Unknown man who talked to Diana at 1:15

KASHVI STARTED DRAWING red lines to connect this to what was already on the wall. "The timing suggests the contamination happened between twelve-forty-five and one-fifteen," I said. "Either at Frontier Burgers, or someone added peanut oil to her food while she was at the picnic table."

"Or the man who talked to her gave her something," Anthone suggested. "Maybe offered her a drink or a snack that was contaminated."

"But why would she accept food from someone if she had a deadly allergy?" Jet asked.

"Maybe she trusted him," Cassidey said quietly. "If it was family, she might not have thought to be careful."

The room fell silent again as the implications sank in.

"We need to find David Sterling," I said finally. "And we need to have another conversation with Jake Webb."

"Carefully," Kashvi warned. "If either of them is our killer, we don't want to spook them into running."

"Or into doing something desperate," Anthone added.

I checked my watch. It was almost four o'clock. "Let's call George and share what we've learned. Then we can decide on next steps."

## 21

I woke the next morning to my phone buzzing insistently on the nightstand. Macchiato, who had been laying on my feet as a personal heating pad, gave me an accusatory look that clearly said "your noisy device is interrupting my sleep schedule."

"Sorry, your majesty," I mumbled, reaching for the phone. The caller ID showed George's number. What could be so important he was calling at five AM?

"Eliza?" His voice sounded tired but relieved. "Good news. The lab results came back clean for all the food vendors. No peanut contamination in any of the samples we collected."

I sat up, suddenly wide awake. "That's wonderful! Does this mean we can reopen?" If it was, we had time to get breakfast on the grill.

"As of this morning, yes. Delia will send you the official clearance paperwork, but you're free to resume normal operations."

"Thank you, George. This is such a relief." And it was—

not just for the financial pressure, but for my team's morale and our reputation in the community.

"There's something else," he said, his tone shifting to more serious. "I need to ask you about your... information gathering yesterday. Word gets around in a small town."

I winced. Of course Martha would have mentioned our visit, probably to half the town by now. "We were just trying to understand what happened."

"I know. And normally I'd tell you to leave it to the professionals, but you might have stumbled onto something important. Can you come in this morning? Bring Anthone and that girl—Cassidey. I want to get her full statement about what she saw after the screaming started."

"Of course. What time?" I rubbed my eyes and imagined the warm bitterness of my first cup of coffee.

"How about ten? That gives you time to get the diner reopened first." He paused and I heard noise in the background, the bustle of a busy investigation. "Actually, on second thought, why don't I come to you? Might be less intimidating for the girl if we do this in familiar surroundings rather than at the station."

After we hung up, I immediately called the team group chat. Within minutes, my phone was buzzing with excited responses from Jacquie, Will, Lissa, and Anthone. Even Cassidey, who I'd added to the group yesterday, sent back a string of happy face emojis.

By six-thirty, I was at EB Eats, and the energy was infectious. Jacquie was already firing up the grill smiling like she'd reunited with a beloved friend. Will and Lissa were setting up the dining room, and Anthone was chopping cilantro with the precision of an experienced prep cook.

"Where do you want me to start?" Cassidey asked,

appearing at my elbow with an eagerness that made my heart happy.

It was too soon for her to pick up a knife and prep—she'd start there when we officially hired her. Until then I didn't want her cutting herself. "How about you help Lissa get the coffee station ready?" I suggested. "We'll probably have a rush once word gets out that we're open again."

She nodded and hurried off, and I noticed how naturally she moved through the space now. Just a few days ago, she'd been tentative and scared. This morning, she looked like she belonged.

"You thinking of making it official?" Jacquie asked, following my gaze.

"The thought had crossed my mind," I admitted. "She's a hard worker, and she's good with customers." Everything else was a matter of training.

"Plus, she needs us," Jacquie said with the practical wisdom of someone who'd raised three kids. "And sometimes that's reason enough."

By nine-fifteen, we were ready to open—a little more than two hours late, but still early enough for pancakes. I unlocked the front door and flipped the sign to "Open," then stepped back to survey my little kingdom. The diner gleamed, the coffee smelled perfect, bacon was on the flat-top, and my team was ready for whatever the day brought.

Our first customer was Woody Howell, who shuffled in with a grin that made him look twenty years younger.

"Heard you were back in business," he said, settling onto his usual stool at the counter. "Figured I'd better get here before the breakfast rush."

"Good thinking," I said, pouring his coffee before he even asked. "The usual?"

"You bet. And make it a double—I've been surviving on my own cooking for two days."

Lissa laughed as she took his order to the kitchen. "How did that go?"

"Terrible," Woody said with mock seriousness. "I burned toast, overcooked eggs, and somehow managed to make coffee that tasted like motor oil. I think the cats next door have been avoiding my kitchen window just from the smell."

Within an hour, we had a steady stream of customers—some genuinely needing breakfast, others clearly just wanting to show support and hear the latest gossip. I noticed several people making a point of ordering more than they usually did, and I suspected Nueva Vida was rallying around us in the way small towns do when one of their own faces trouble. If I was right, then the other restaurants would be doing banner business as soon as they opened.

Alistair McKay burst through the door just before ten like he was making a grand entrance on stage, his voice already raised before he'd even cleared the threshold.

"I suppose you think this clears you of all suspicion!" he announced to the entire diner, spreading his arms wide as he surveyed the room. Several customers looked up from their breakfasts with resigned expressions, some with smiles, eager to witness one of Alistair's performances.

I took a deep breath and reminded myself that banning customers was bad for business, even when those customers were theatrical pains in the neck. And, let's be honest, Alistair would never eat here.

"It clears everyone of accidental contamination," I said evenly, continuing to wipe down the counter while he claimed the center of the dining room like it was his personal stage. "The food was safe."

"But someone still killed that woman!" he declared, spinning to face the other customers as if addressing a jury. "Someone who knew exactly what they were doing! Someone who planned it!"

"The police are investigating," I said, hoping to end his monologue before it gained momentum.

"Are they, though?" Alistair whirled back toward me, his voice carrying to every corner of the diner. "Because I heard you've been gallivanting around town, playing detective again! Asking questions! Interfering with official business!"

I felt heat rise in my cheeks as every customer in the place turned to look at me. "We're just trying to help."

"Well, you might want to be more careful about who you help!" he proclaimed, gesturing dramatically toward the kitchen where I could see Cassidey through the pass-through. "Some people aren't as innocent as they pretend to be! Some people have connections to violence and criminal activity!"

Before I could respond to that inflammatory accusation, the door chimed and George walked in, his badge out marking this as official business. His timing couldn't have been better.

"Morning, Eliza," he said calmly, then turned toward the center of the room where Alistair was still holding court. "Alistair."

"Detective!" Alistair practically shouted, clearly delighted to have law enforcement witness his dramatic revelations. "I was just telling everyone that they should be careful about the company they keep!"

George's expression didn't change, but I saw something dangerous flicker in his eyes. "What kind of company would that be?"

Alistair gestured wildly toward the kitchen again. "Well,

that girl she's got working here! The one with the gang connections! People are talking, Detective! When someone dies under suspicious circumstances, maybe we should look at the people who have experience with violence!"

I felt my protective instincts flare like a match struck in the dark. "Cassidey is sixteen years old and deserves a chance to start her life. Anyone who has a problem with that can take it up with me."

"Are you making a formal accusation, Alistair?" George asked, his voice taking on the kind of authoritative edge that made it clear he was done with the theatrics.

Alistair's dramatic posture deflated slightly. "I'm just making an observation, Detective."

"Then observe quietly," George said firmly. "Or better yet, observe from your own establishment."

Alistair gathered what remained of his dignity and stormed toward the door, pausing only to deliver one final proclamation: "Mark my words—the truth will come out!" The door slammed behind him with enough force to rattle the windows.

"Sorry about that," I said once he was gone. "Some people just can't resist stirring up trouble. I never know how to handle him beyond letting the rant run out. I can't imagine he'd take a laugh well."

"Don't worry about Alistair," George said, settling onto a stool at the end of the counter. "He's been making noise about Cassidey since yesterday. I wanted to address it before it gets out of hand."

"Is she really a suspect?" I asked, keeping my voice low.

"Everyone's a suspect until they're not," George said diplomatically. "But no, I don't think a sixteen-year-old girl with no connection to the victim randomly decided to commit murder with peanut oil. Denise disagrees with me, but then again, Denise thinks everyone's guilty until proven innocent."

I poured him coffee and slid it across the counter. "Speaking of the investigation, we gathered some information yesterday that you might find useful."

"So I heard." George's smile was wry. "Martha Hendricks gave me a very detailed report of your visit to the post office. According to her, you've identified David Sterling as the victim's ex-husband and his son Jake as a potential witness."

"Jake lied to us about knowing Diana," I said. "And he was checking on his father's whereabouts right after she was found dead."

George nodded. "We're looking into both of them. David Sterling seems to have disappeared right after the fair, and Jake Webb has been evasive when we've tried to interview him."

"Have you found David's truck?" Anthone asked, as he placed a plate of eggs Benedict on the passthrough making my mouth water.

"Not yet," George said. "But we've put out a BOLO. He can't have gone far—his bank account shows he doesn't have much money for an extended trip. His cards haven't been used. And I'm not telling you anything else."

I thought about Ruth Morrison's comments about David scraping by after the divorce. Even if George meant it, I couldn't hold out on him in retaliation. "Maybe he's not running. Maybe he's hiding."

"Or maybe he's dead too," George said grimly. "If Jake Webb killed his stepmother for money, he might have killed his father to cover his tracks."

The thought sent a chill through me. We'd been thinking of this as a single murder, but what if it was the beginning of something larger?

"George," I said carefully, "when you interview Cassidey, please remember she's just a kid. She's been through enough already."

"I'll be gentle," he promised. "But I need to know exactly what she saw. It might be the key to solving this whole thing."

As if summoned by our conversation, Cassidey appeared from the back of the diner, looking nervous but determined. Jacquie was right behind her, wiping her hands on her apron.

"Detective Kramer?" Cassidey said politely. "Eliza said you wanted to talk to me?"

"Just George is fine," he said with a smile that transformed his serious face. "And yes, I'd like to hear about what you saw yesterday after the screaming started. Since you're a minor, you'll need an adult present. Would Jacquie be okay, or would you prefer Eliza?"

"Jacquie's fine," Cassidey said, glancing back at the older woman with something like affection. "She's been teaching me things all morning."

"Perfect," Jacquie said. "Eliza, can you handle the kitchen for a few minutes? Anthone's got everything under control, but just in case we get a rush."

I nodded and watched as George led them to a quiet booth, noting how he positioned himself to seem less intimidating. I don't know where Denise Collett learned her methods, but George understood how to talk to people who didn't trust authority figures.

## 22

I tried to stay busy while George interviewed Cassidey, but I found myself wiping the same section of prep counter for the third time while straining to hear their conversation through the passthrough. From what I could catch, George was being as gentle as promised, asking open-ended questions and giving Cassidey time to think.

"She's doing fine," Lissa said quietly, appearing beside me with a fresh pot of coffee. "Look at her body language. She's sitting up straight, making eye contact. That's not someone who's scared."

She was right. Cassidey looked more confident than I'd ever seen her, answering questions without shaking or looking away. Jacquie was nodding encouragingly and occasionally asking clarifying questions that helped Cassidey remember more details.

The lunch rush was starting to build—word had definitely gotten out that we were reopened, and more than one person made a point of telling me how glad they were to have us back. It reminded me why I'd fallen in love with

Nueva Vida in the first place. In a small town, your neighbors became your extended family, for better or worse.

"Eliza?" George called from the booth. "Could you join us for a minute?"

I checked that Anthone was in control of the orders before I walked over. Jacquie stood up to let me slide into the booth.

"That was beautifully handled, Detective," Jacquie said quietly. "You made her feel like her words mattered instead of like she was in trouble. Thank you for that."

George nodded acknowledgment as Jacquie headed back to the kitchen. I could see that Cassidey looked calm but tired—talking about traumatic events, even from the witness perspective, took emotional energy.

"Cassidey's been very helpful," George said as I settled in. "She's given me a much clearer picture of the timeline and what she observed. But I want to make sure I understand something correctly. You might help get the details tied down."

He consulted his notes. "You said you saw someone leaving the picnic area quickly after the screaming started, carrying what might have been a small container?"

Cassidey nodded. "It was hard to see clearly because everyone was moving around, but yes. He was walking fast but trying not to look like he was running."

"Can you tell me anything else about this person? Not just height, clothing, age, but attitude, gait, posture. Was he hunched over, hiding his real height?"

She closed her eyes, concentrating again. "Like I said, maybe average height? Dark clothes—I think jeans and a dark shirt or jacket. It didn't look like he was pretending to be someone else. Like padding his clothes. I didn't get the

feeling he was old, maybe he moved too fast for that? And..."
She paused, frowning and looked to me for support.

"Take your time," George said gently.

"He had a baseball cap on. Dark colored. It made it hard to see his face, but there was something familiar about the way he moved."

"Familiar how?" I asked, trying not to sound too eager.

"Like maybe I'd seen him around town before, but I couldn't place where." She opened her eyes and looked at George. "It's hard to remember anything more. I'm sorry I can't be more specific."

"You're doing great," George assured her. "This is exactly the kind of detail that helps us build a complete picture."

My phone buzzed with a text message. I glanced at it and saw it was from Kashvi: *Jake Webb just came into the store. Buying a map and asking about bus schedules. Seemed really nervous and kept looking over his shoulder. Also had a bag full of camping supplies. Thought you should know.*

I showed the message to George, who frowned thoughtfully.

"Interesting," he said. "Though there could be innocent explanations for all of that."

"Such as?" I asked, if we were right, then he was looking pretty suspicious.

"Well, if he thinks his father might be in trouble, he could be planning to look for him," George said closing his notebook. "The camping supplies suggest he might be thinking David's hiding out somewhere in the wilderness. And if he's scared because he thinks there's a killer loose in town, being nervous makes sense."

I hadn't considered that angle. "So he might be trying to help his father rather than run away?"

"It's possible. Despite what Martha told you about them

not getting along, family dynamics can be complicated. Sometimes the people who fight the most are the ones who'll drop everything to help each other when it really matters. And we follow proof, not suspicions. It's too easy to see things that support a theory and miss facts that don't fit."

That gave me pause. I thought about my own complicated relationship with my ex-husband—I'd hated him toward the end, but if he'd been in real danger, I probably would have tried to help. Maybe if he'd talked to me, he'd still be alive. In jail but still living.

"Have you been able to locate David Sterling?" I asked.

"That's... complicated," George said. "We found his truck abandoned up in the hills, but there's no sign of foul play. No blood, no evidence of struggle, no body. It looks like he parked it there deliberately and walked away."

"Why would he do that?"

George glanced around to make sure no one else was listening, then lowered his voice. "I can't tell you details of the investigation."

"But if it helps keep us safe," I didn't want to play on our budding relationship to get him to tell me. "You know we can't stop hearing clues, right. Everyone is counting on us to find the killer."

"That doesn't mean you have to act on it." He gave me a stern look that he spoiled with a smile. "Yeah, I know you won't stop. So, we've been digging into David Sterling's recent activities. Turns out he's been involved in some questionable financial dealings since moving to Nueva Vida. Nothing violent, but potentially illegal. Securities fraud, maybe some kind of investment scam."

Like Peter Trent, our last case—okay our first.

"So he might be hiding because he's afraid of getting

arrested?" Cassidey asked. I felt bad that we hadn't let her go back to the kitchen. She didn't need to hear any of this.

"Or because he owes money to the wrong people," George said grimly. "When Diana came to town, she might have been planning to expose him, or threaten to report him to authorities. That could have given him motive to kill her."

"But, still, why would Jake be buying camping supplies?" I asked.

"Maybe Jake doesn't know about his father's illegal activities. Maybe he thinks David is just scared and hiding, and he wants to help."

I found myself reassessing everything we thought we knew. "So Jake could be innocent?"

"It's possible he's just a worried son trying to find his missing father," George said. "Though he definitely lied about knowing Diana, which makes him look suspicious."

"People lie for all sorts of reasons," Cassidey said quietly. "Sometimes you lie because you're scared, not because you're guilty."

George and I both looked at her, struck by the wisdom in that observation. My heart clenched at the idea she knew so much about the dark side of life at such a young age.

"That's very true," George said. "Jake might have lied because he was afraid we'd automatically suspect him due to the family connection." He stood and stuck his notebook in his pocket. "I need to update the files with this. If you think of anything else, call me, don't go haring off into danger."

## 23

A fter George left to follow up on Jake's activities, I sat in the booth with Cassidey for a few minutes, letting the normal sounds of the busy diner wash over us. The clatter of cutlery against plates, and faint hiss of food hitting the hot flattop was like meditation music to me.

"How do you feel?" I asked.

"Good, actually," she said, and I could hear the surprise in her voice. "I was scared at first, but Detective Kramer made it feel like we were just having a conversation. Like my information actually mattered."

"It does matter. You might have given them important evidence." I thought back to her comments about talking to the police when we were at the fair. "What does this mean for you and the gang?"

"I thought about what you told me. He thinks keeping the cops away is worth it. Told me he wouldn't come after me, but I'd owe him," she said. "Do you really think Jake Webb might be innocent?"

Owe him what? She didn't seem concerned so I let it go.

"I don't know," I said honestly. "But George made a good point about family relationships being complicated. Maybe Jake and his father care about each other more than they let on."

"The way he was moving when I saw him leaving the picnic area—if that was him," she said thoughtfully, "It reminded me of gang members trying to avoid attention. But thinking about it now, it could have been someone who was just scared and confused, trying to get away from something horrible without looking suspicious."

That observation gave me even more pause. We'd been so focused on seeing guilt in Jake's behavior that we might have missed signs of fear or panic. "We should get back to work. Feeding people is more important than doing George's job. Follow Will around so you learn to bus tables."

The lunch rush was slowing down when Vic walked in, still wearing his fire department uniform. He caught my eye and gestured toward the counter, so I left Cassidey, who'd graduated from bus girl to server for her training, to help Lissa with customers and went to greet him.

"Heard you're back in business," he said, accepting the coffee I poured for him. "How does it feel?"

"Like coming home," I said. "Though I could do without all the murder and investigation drama."

"Speaking of which," he said, lowering his voice, "there's something you should know. We got called out about an hour ago to investigate a possible structure fire up in the hills. Turned out to be a false alarm, but we found David Sterling's truck hidden in some trees off service road 12."

"George mentioned you'd found it. Any new details?" I didn't feel guilty for asking. Despite what George wanted, I didn't promise him anything about stopping my investigation.

"Well, here's the interesting thing—we also found evidence of a recent campsite nearby. Someone had been staying there, probably for at least a day or two. Left behind some food containers and a sleeping bag."

Interesting and more than what I already knew. I made a mental note to text this to Kashvi. "David?"

"Most likely. And it looks like he was camping up there voluntarily. I know there's a theory he's the killer, but he'd be crazy to hide out so close to town, right?"

"So he might still be alive?" I blurted it out at the sudden thought he'd been murdered too. We didn't need another body added to the complications of this case.

"Very likely. Though why he's hiding is still the question." Vic took a sip of his coffee. "Could be fear of whoever killed Diana. Could be guilt over something else entirely."

I thought about George's revelation regarding David's possible financial crimes. "What if Diana came to town not just to talk to him, but to confront him about something illegal he'd been doing?"

"That would certainly give him motive," Vic agreed. "But it would also explain why he's hiding now—maybe he's afraid of being arrested for whatever Diana was going to expose."

"And Jake might be trying to find him to warn him or help him." Something that dire would override any petty family disagreements.

"Family loyalty can make people do unexpected things," Vic said, almost echoing my thoughts. "Even families that seem dysfunctional from the outside."

Vic left after that and I stood there starring out the front window. The afternoon sun slanted through the windows, and I realized that sometimes the most dangerous assumption is thinking you understand people's motivations.

Maybe Jake Webb wasn't a killer covering his tracks—maybe he was just a son afraid of losing the only family he had left.

## 24

I was chatting with Jacquie as she made an order of five breakfasts for the family in the corner booth — breakfast all day was a favorite for tourists. Business was good and I could almost forget about the murder—almost. The pleasant vibe was broken when Emily Stonehouse came through the door looking more frazzled than I'd ever seen her. Emily owned Nueva Vida's largest tourist gift shop and usually maintained the kind of polished appearance that suggested everything in her life was under perfect control. Today, her blond hair was pulled back in a messy ponytail, and she kept glancing over her shoulder like she expected to be followed.

"Eliza," she said, sliding into a corner booth, "I need to talk to you. About the fair, about Diana Whitfield."

I poured her coffee and settled across from her. "What's on your mind?"

"I think I might be in trouble," she said, her voice barely above a whisper. "That detective—the woman, Collett—she's been asking questions about me. About my business."

"What kind of questions?"

Emily wrapped her hands around her coffee mug like it was an anchor. "About money. About whether I've been having financial problems. About whether I knew Diana Whitfield before the fair."

That last question caught my attention. "Did you know her?"

Emily shuddered. "That's the thing—I think I might have. Not personally, but... she came into my shop about a month ago. I didn't think anything of it at the time, just another tourist looking at pottery and jewelry. But she asked a lot of questions about local businesses, about who owned what, about how long people had been in town."

"That does sound like more than casual tourist interest," I said.

"And she bought something," Emily continued, looking increasingly agitated. "A turquoise necklace. Paid cash, but she asked for a receipt with my full business information. Said she might want to write a review online."

I leaned forward. "Emily, why didn't you mention this to the police earlier?"

"Because I didn't remember at first! You know how many tourists come through the shop. They all blur together after a while." She swallowed and I wonder what was causing so much fear. There was more than just forgetting to tell the police something. "But then Detective Collett started asking about my finances, and I got nervous and tried to remember if there was any reason she'd be focusing on me, and that's when I remembered the woman with all the questions."

"What did you tell Detective Collett about your finances?" Was that the real reason she was so worried?

Emily's face flushed red. "The truth. That I've been struggling. That I owe money. That I've been trying some new business ventures to make ends meet."

There was something in her tone that suggested she wasn't telling me everything. "What kind of business ventures?"

"Multi-level marketing," she said, looking embarrassed. "I know how it sounds, but I was desperate. Essential oils, weight loss supplements, jewelry parties. I even tried selling insurance for a while."

"Emily, that's not illegal. Why would Detective Collett care about that?" I remembered being told about Emily's shady deals before. They'd turned out to be normal home sales ventures. I guess anything was shady to some people.

"I might have oversold the potential earning opportunity to some people. And I might have used money I owed up the line to encourage people to sign up?"

My heart sank. That sounded dangerously close to fraud, even if Emily hadn't intended it that way.

"How much money are we talking about?" I asked.

"About ten thousand dollars," she said miserably. "I kept thinking I could turn it around, that the next venture would be the one that really took off and I could pay everyone back. But instead, I just kept digging myself deeper."

"And you think Diana Whitfield somehow found out about this?"

"I don't know! But what if she wasn't just a tourist? What if she was investigating local businesses for some reason? What if she was planning to expose me?"

The possibility sent chills through me. If Diana had been investigating financial irregularities in Nueva Vida, it would explain why she'd stayed for a week and asked so many questions.

"Have you told George about this?" I asked.

"Not yet. I'm scared, Eliza. If word gets out about the money problems, I'll lose everything. The shop, my reputation, maybe even my freedom if they decide to press charges."

I studied Emily's face, trying to read the emotions there. Fear, definitely. Guilt, certainly. But was there something else? Desperation could make people do terrible things. "Emily, where were you when Diana collapsed at the fair?"

"At my booth, selling jewelry and crafts—another way to get money to fix my mistake. I had customers the whole time—you can ask them." She pulled out her phone and started scrolling through photos. "Look, I even have pictures from that afternoon. Customers posting on social media about their purchases."

She showed me several Instagram posts timestamped during the crucial period, all with Emily smiling with various customers at her booth. It seemed like solid alibi evidence, but social media timestamps could be manipulated.

"The thing is," Emily continued, "I keep thinking about that necklace she bought. What if it wasn't just a random purchase? What if she was marking me somehow, like a reminder to herself to investigate my business?"

"You're probably overthinking this," I said, though I wasn't entirely convinced. "But you should definitely tell George everything. Hiding information will only make you look more suspicious."

After Emily left, looking marginally less panicked but still worried, I found myself thinking about her story. Diana Whitfield had been asking questions about local businesses a month before her death. That suggested a level of curiosity that went beyond reaching out to visit her ex-husband.

## 25

K ashvi sent a text to say her helper, Mallory, was taking over and she'd come for coffee and an update.

"You look like you've heard something interesting," she said, settling into the booth Emily had vacated.

I filled her in on Emily's confession, watching Kashvi's expression grow more intrigued with each detail.

"So Diana might have been investigating multiple people in Nueva Vida," Kashvi said when I finished. "Not just her ex-husband."

"It's starting to look that way. The question is why. Was she some kind of private investigator? A journalist? Or just someone with a lot of time and money who enjoyed exposing fraud?"

"I can look into her background more deeply. One of the mystery books in the store should have a plot that will help." She held up a hand to stop my objection. "I know they are fiction, but the authors must do research, right? I can see if Diana had any connection to law enforcement or financial investigation. Go a bit deeper on the social media research."

I gave up. After all, I was a diner owner, not a trained investigator, so who was I to judge when people took up a hobby. "That would be helpful. And we should probably tell George about Emily's confession, even though she's planning to do it herself."

"Absolutely. Though I have to say, Emily Stonehouse running a Ponzi scheme isn't exactly what I expected when we started investigating this murder." She giggled at the idea of Emily pulling a Bernie Madoff.

"There's something else," I said. "Emily's story makes me wonder who else Diana might have been investigating. If she was asking questions about local businesses, she might have discovered other financial irregularities."

Kashvi took a long sip of her iced coffee. "Like what?"

"I don't know. But think about it—a small tourist town with seasonal businesses, people struggling to make ends meet, limited oversight from state or federal authorities. It would be easy for financial crimes to go unnoticed."

Kashvi was already making notes. "It's definitely hard to run a business and if you aren't careful, a little cheating can be a gateway. We should look at other places that have been struggling. See if anyone else had contact with Diana before the fair."

I didn't know how she'd find out which businesses were possibly doing something with their finances. "I guess this opens up a whole new theory. I don't like how this keeps getting more complicated."

Yesterday's rain had cleaned the air, now the sun was baking us again, but I found myself feeling cold despite the warmth. If Diana had been killed to silence an investigation, then her murderer was someone with a lot to lose—and possibly a lot more to hide.

"Kashvi," I said slowly, "what if we've been thinking

about this all wrong? What if Diana's death wasn't about her ex-husband or family drama at all? What if it was about business?"

She finished her coffee while she thought about the question. "You mean Jake and David Sterling might be innocent?"

"I mean we might have multiple people with motives we haven't even discovered yet."

As if summoned by our conversation, the door chimed and Bernie Castro from Frontier Burgers walked in, looking like he hadn't slept well. He approached our table with the hesitant manner of someone who needed to confess something but didn't want to.

"Eliza," he said, "I heard Emily Stonehouse was here earlier. If she was talking about Diana Whitfield, there's something you should know."

Kashvi and I exchanged glances. "What's that, Bernie?"

"Diana came to my restaurant about three weeks ago. Not for food—for a meeting. She said she was writing an article about small-town economics and wanted to interview local business owners about their experiences."

"Did you do the interview?" I asked. Was he here because Emily sent him? I needed to put a stop to the idea I was some kind of screening step before talking to the real investigators.

Bernie's expression was grim. "I did. And I might have told her some things I shouldn't have. About the struggles of running a small restaurant, about the creative ways we sometimes have to handle finances to stay afloat. About the gray areas between legal and illegal when you're just trying to survive. You know how easy it is to keep griping when someone is willing to listen."

My stomach dropped. Kashvi didn't need to go searching

for businesses, they were coming to us. "What kind of gray areas, Bernie?"

"Tax issues. Cash transactions that might not get reported properly. Paying some employees under the table to avoid payroll taxes. The kind of things that could get you in serious trouble if the wrong people found out."

And now Diana Whitfield was dead, taking whatever information she'd gathered to the grave.

"Bernie," I said carefully, "do you think Diana was really writing an article?"

"I don't know," he said. "But I keep thinking about the questions she asked. They were very specific, very detailed. Like she already knew what she was looking for and just needed confirmation."

As Bernie left, promising to talk to George later that day, I realized our investigation had just gotten a lot more complicated. We weren't just looking for one killer with one motive—we were potentially looking at multiple people with financial crimes to hide.

"This changes everything," Kashvi said quietly.

"Yes, it does. The question is: how many secrets was Diana Whitfield planning to expose? Why did she breeze into town to dig out people's skeletons. And how many people were willing to kill to stop her?"

## 26

I was wiping down the counter for what felt like the hundredth time the next morning, my mind still on the chaos that had greeted me at home earlier— Macchiato had knocked over my bedroom flower arrangement in what I was pretty sure was retaliation for my late arrival last night, leaving water and petals scattered across the hardwood floor. The familiar sounds of the busy diner —the sizzle of bacon on Jacquie's grill, the cheerful chatter of customers, and the rich aroma of fresh coffee—helped push the morning's domestic disaster to the back of my mind.

The bell over the door gave a tinkle and when I looked up, George walked in with a woman I didn't recognize, both of them wearing the kind of serious expressions that meant business rather than breakfast.

"Eliza," George said, "I'd like you to meet Sarah Martinez. She's been helping us understand Diana Whitfield's background."

The woman was probably in her thirties, with short

auburn hair and the kind of sharp, observant eyes that reminded me of Kashvi when she was working on a particularly interesting story for her book blog.

"Ms. Burton," Sarah said, extending her hand with a warm smile. "George tells me you've been very helpful with the investigation."

"Just trying to understand what happened," I said, shaking her hand. "Can I get you coffee? Something to eat?"

"Coffee would be wonderful," she said, settling onto a counter stool. "It's been a long morning."

I poured coffee for both of them, noting how Sarah seemed to be studying the diner with careful attention— taking in the details of our setup, the flow of customers, the casual interactions between staff and regulars.

"Sarah has some background information about Diana that might help explain why she was in Nueva Vida," George said carefully.

"Beyond visiting her ex-husband?" I asked.

"Diana worked as a forensic accountant," Sarah said, adding cream to her coffee with the precise movements of someone who liked things done exactly right. "She specialized in identifying financial irregularities in small businesses."

"You mean like tax problems?" I asked, thinking about Bernie's confession yesterday and Emily's Ponzi scheme worries.

"Tax issues, yes, but also investment fraud, unreported income, falsified records. The kinds of problems that can develop when businesses are struggling and owners get creative with their accounting."

I felt a little chill of recognition. "Was she investigating businesses here in Nueva Vida?"

George shifted uncomfortably, but Sarah leaned forward

with interest. "We think so. We found notes in her hotel room suggesting she'd been looking into several local operations."

"Including some of the food vendors from the fair?" I asked.

"Possibly," Sarah said, while George shot her a warning look. "We're still reviewing her research, but any information from the community would be helpful. That's why I'm here. You've already sent people on her list to the police station. I'm hope more of them will confide in you."

Was I supposed to become the official gatekeeper of confessions?

The door chimed, and Kashvi walked in with her usual perfect timing, stopping short when she saw our serious gathering. "Sorry," she said, "I didn't realize you were having an important conversation."

"It's fine," I said. "Sarah was just explaining that Diana was some kind of financial investigator."

Kashvi's eyes lit up with interest. "Really? That's fascinating. So she wasn't just a tourist after all."

I liked the fact that she kept our knowledge secret. I mean George and Sarah knew, but Kashvi didn't know they knew?

"No, she was quite skilled at what she did," Sarah said. "Diana had a reputation for being very thorough and very discreet. She could spend weeks in a community, gathering information, without anyone realizing what she was really doing."

"Until someone figured it out," I said quietly. Had she gotten sloppy? Did her ex know what her job entailed?

"Exactly," George said. "And that person might have decided Diana was too dangerous to let live."

"But how would they have known?" Kashvi asked,

pulling out her notebook never willing to miss an opportunity to gather information. "If she was so good at being discreet?"

"That's what we're trying to figure out," Sarah said. "Diana was supposed to be very careful about maintaining her cover."

"Maybe someone recognized her from a previous investigation?" I suggested. "Or maybe she asked one too many specific questions?"

"Both possibilities," George agreed. "We're hoping to piece together her activities over the past months to see where her cover might have been blown. She must have stayed somewhere when she first started this. I'd also be interested if her ex or her stepson met with her."

Emily Stonehouse chose that moment to walk in, looking like she'd spent another sleepless night. She approached our group with the determined air of someone who'd made a difficult decision.

"Detective Kramer," she said, "I've been thinking about what I told Eliza yesterday. About my financial problems and Diana's visit to my shop. I think I should probably tell you everything officially."

George nodded. "That would be helpful, Emily. Why don't we schedule a time for you to come to the station?"

"I appreciate you coming forward," Sarah added warmly. "It takes courage to be honest when you're worried about potential consequences."

Emily managed a weak smile. "Eliza helped me realize that being honest was better than living in fear. At least now I know Diana was investigating multiple businesses, not just targeting me specifically."

"That's right," I said. "You're not alone in this, Emily."

Emily left us with a lighter step, her back straight and stride confident. Unburdening herself had lifted some of her fear. And an appointment to confess everything to the authorities in three hours.

"See? Community support makes all the difference," Sarah said looking at George with a smile. "People are much more likely to cooperate when they feel like they're helping rather than being accused."

"I know," he said on a sigh. "Maybe you could give Denise the same advice. That doesn't mean I'm agreeing to you, Kashvi, and Jet getting yourselves into danger, Eliza."

"Here's the pattern we've been seeing," Sarah said returning to the topic. "Diana would identify businesses that might be having financial difficulties, then engage the owners in casual conversation to gather more information."

"How many businesses was she looking into?" Kashvi asked. I could see she wanted to start listing names. Fodder for our murder board, and maybe the detail we needed to identify a real suspect.

"Based on her notes, at least a dozen in Nueva Vida," Sarah said. "She was very thorough."

I felt my stomach drop. A dozen businesses in a town this size meant Diana had been investigating a significant portion of the local economy.

"Sarah," I said carefully, "do you think Diana was killed by someone she was investigating?"

"It's certainly possible. If someone discovered what she was really doing, they might have felt desperate enough to stop her permanently."

"But that would mean the killer is still here," Kashvi said. "Still operating their business, still interacting with the community like nothing happened."

"Yes," George said grimly. "And they're probably watching to see how much we know about Diana's investigation."

The thought sent chills through me. I looked around my diner, thinking about all the customers I served every day. How many of them might have secrets worth killing for?

"George," I said, "should we be worried about our safety? If someone killed Diana to protect their financial crimes, they might see us as threats too."

"Just be careful," he said. "Don't go anywhere alone, and call immediately if anything seems suspicious."

After George and Sarah left, Kashvi and I sat in the quiet diner, processing what we'd learned. Jacquie called out an order of brownies that had our name on it.

"This explains a lot," Kashvi said after taking a huge bite of the treat. "Why Diana was in town for a week, why she was asking so many questions, why someone might have wanted her dead."

"It also means we might have been looking at this all wrong," I said. "We've been focused on Jake Webb and David Sterling, but the real killer might be someone we serve coffee to every morning."

"Someone who's been watching us investigate, knowing that we might stumble across the same information Diana found."

I thought about Emily's nervousness, Bernie's confessions, all the other business owners who'd seemed on edge since Diana's death.

"Kashvi," I said slowly, "what if we make a list of everyone Diana might have been investigating? Cross-reference it with who had access to peanut oil and opportunity at the fair?"

"That's a good idea. But isn't peanut oil just a regular

grocery item? I have to say, thinking about our neighbors and friends as potential murderers is depressing."

"Isn't that small-town life," I said with a bitter laugh. "Where everyone knows everyone else's business, but nobody knows anyone's secrets."

As if to prove my point, the door chimed and Pearl Sargent walked in, looking more worried than I'd seen her since her husband's heart attack two years ago.

"Eliza," she said, approaching the counter where Kashvi and I were sitting, "I need to ask you something. That forensic accountant—Diana Whitfield—I think she came to my bakery a couple of weeks ago asking questions."

How did Pearl know Diana's real purpose? If I had to put money on it, the trail went from Betty at the station, to Martha at the post office, and was on its way around the town.

"What kind of questions?" Kashvi asked.

"About my business practices, my suppliers, how I handle payments." Pearl sat down heavily on a stool. "I told her things I probably shouldn't have. About how sometimes I have to be flexible with my accounting when money's tight."

"Pearl," I said gently, "you need to talk to Detective Kramer about this. He and Sarah Martinez are gathering information about all of Diana's business visits."

"But what if I said something that made her think I was committing a crime?" Pearl's voice was rising with anxiety.

"Then it's better to be honest now than to let them find out later," Kashvi said kindly. "From what we've learned, Diana was investigating multiple businesses. You're not alone in this."

After Pearl left, promising to talk to George later, I realized how many people in Nueva Vida might be feeling the same way—scared that Diana had misunderstood their harmless business practices and reported them as criminal activity.

"The question is," Kashvi said, "which one of them was scared enough to commit murder?"

## 27

The lunch rush was picking up when Vic arrived, still in his fire department uniform but with the relaxed posture of someone who'd just successfully dealt with a minor emergency. Lissa was cheerfully taking orders while Will cleared tables with the methodical efficiency Jacquie and I had trained into him. The familiar rhythm of the busy diner—clinking silverware, friendly chatter, the occasional laugh from a corner booth—helped ease some of the tension from our morning revelations.

"Please tell me you have good news," I said, pouring Vic's usual coffee while he settled onto a stool between Kashvi and me.

"Depends on your definition of good," he said, accepting the steaming mug gratefully. "We got called out to what looked like a small brush fire up near where David Sterling's truck was found. Turned out to be a false alarm, but we found more evidence that someone's been camping in the area."

"David?" Kashvi asked, looking up from her notebook

where she'd been organizing our growing list of potential suspects. "What kind of evidence?"

"Most likely, him. Not too many people camp out this time of year—too much danger of flash floods. We found a fresh campfire, recently used sleeping area, some food containers. Whoever it is, they're staying well-hidden but they're alive and managing okay."

"That's something, at least," I said, refilling the coffee pot from the machine. "Any sign of Jake Webb looking for him?"

"Funny you should ask," Vic said, watching Lissa expertly balance three plates while taking another order. "We saw tire tracks from what looked like a mountain bike on some of the trails. Recent tracks, probably from yesterday or this morning."

"So Jake might have been up there searching for his father?"

"Could be. Or could be any number of people who use those trails for recreation." Vic took a sip of coffee and studied our faces. "You two look like you've been having serious conversations."

I filled him in on our morning visit from Sarah Martinez and what we'd learned about Diana's forensic accounting work, keeping my voice low so the other customers wouldn't overhear. The last thing Nueva Vida needed was more gossip about the investigation.

"So she was investigating financial irregularities," Vic said thoughtfully. "That explains why she was asking so many detailed questions about local businesses—I get the gossip too. And no one would spread that news. 'Hey, I'm being investigated by the IRS—isn't that interesting?'"

"And why someone might have wanted to stop her," Kashvi added, then looked up as the door chimed.

June Spenser from Outdoor Experiences walked in,

looking around the diner uncertainly before approaching the counter. June usually exuded the kind of outdoorsy confidence that came from spending most of her time hiking and camping with tourists, but today she seemed hesitant, almost nervous.

The diner was becoming information central for business owners today. Normally the bell rang all day as hungry diners entered. Today? Every time I heard it, I expected another worried friend to walk in.

"Hi, Eliza," she said, glancing at our little group with obvious curiosity. "Could I get a sandwich to go? Turkey and Swiss, if you have it."

"Of course," I said, writing the order on a slip and passing it through the kitchen window to Anthone who was covering Jacquie's break. It was a bit of a relief that June came to order lunch and not to tell me things she should tell George or Denise. "How's the tour business going?"

"Good, mostly," June said, then continued to look over at our discussion. After a moment, she seemed to make a decision. "You folks look like you're talking about something important. Mind if I ask what's going on? Is it about the murder?"

Vic and Kashvi exchanged glances with me. June had always been observant—it was part of what made her good at running outdoor tours—and she clearly had something on her mind. And I was wrong about why she came in. The sandwich was just an excuse.

"We were just discussing the investigation," I said carefully. "Trying to understand what happened to Diana Whitfield."

June's expression shifted to something that looked like relief mixed with anxiety. "Actually," she said, moving closer and lowering her voice, "that's kind of why I'm here. I keep thinking I should talk to Detective Kramer, but I'm not sure if what I know is important or not."

"What kind of thing?" Kashvi asked.

June looked around to make sure no other customers were within earshot, then leaned against the counter. "Diana hired my company for several private tours over the past month. Not regular tourist tours—she wanted to see specific things."

"What kind of specific things?" Vic asked, giving her a reassuring smile.

"She was interested in observing local businesses. Especially ones that handle a lot of cash—restaurants, shops, service companies. She'd have me drive her past places during busy times so she could watch how they operated."

I felt a familiar chill of a breakthrough on the horizon. "Did she say why she was interested?"

"She told me she was doing research for a book about small-town economics. But the questions she asked..." June shook her head, her ponytail swinging. "They were very focused. About which businesses seemed to be doing better than expected, which owners had recently made expensive purchases, which places always seemed busy but might not be reporting all their income."

"Did you tell anyone about these tours?" I asked, though I suspected I already knew the answer. In Nueva Vida, interesting news had a way of making the rounds.

June's face reddened like a tourist who'd forgotten sunscreen on her first desert hike. "I might have mentioned them to some people. You know how it is—when you have an unusual customer, especially one who tips really well, you talk about it. Now I'm hearing news about her that's kind of scary—that maybe I accidentally put someone on her radar."

"Who specifically did you tell?" Kashvi asked, making notes in her neat handwriting.

"I can't remember everyone. Martha Hendricks at the post office, definitely—she always wants to know about interesting tourists. Some of the other business owners when they asked about my mysterious customer. It seemed like harmless conversation at the time."

Anthone appeared at the kitchen window with June's sandwich, neatly wrapped and ready to go. She paid quickly, clearly eager to leave now that she'd shared her burden.

"I should probably tell Detective Kramer about this," she said, phrasing it more like a question than a statement. Maybe hoping I'd do the dirty work for her.

"Definitely," I agreed. "It might be more important than you realize."

After June left, we sat in contemplative silence for a few minutes, listening to the comfortable sounds of the busy diner around us. Lissa was refilling coffee cups and chatting with the customers, Will was setting up a freshly cleaned table, and the whole place hummed with the kind of community energy that made Nueva Vida feel like home.

"So Diana's cover was blown by small-town gossip," Vic said finally.

"Which means potentially dozens of people knew she was asking suspicious questions about local businesses," I added. "But if she did this for a living, she must have known people talk."

"And if she was investigating financial irregularities, any of those business owners might have decided she was too dangerous to let live," Kashvi finished. "I didn't hear any of this. Eliza we are woefully out of the town grapevine."

Vic's radio crackled to life, summoning him back to the

station for what sounded like a support for an ambulance run.

"I'd better go," he said, standing up and leaving money for his coffee. "George and I aren't exactly friends because of that arson investigation, and here I am stepping into his role by discussing the case with you. Probably better if I don't make things more complicated."

"Be careful out there," I said, giving his hand a quick squeeze.

"You too. If Diana was killed to protect financial secrets, her killer is still out there, probably watching to see how much the investigation has uncovered."

"I wonder if she researched us," Kashvi said. "I don't cut corners, so I'm not worried, but it's weird to think I might have missed her snooping."

"I'm guessing we didn't trip any alarms," I said. "I don't risk penalties by playing around with my reporting."

About ten minutes after Vic left, Denise walked in during a brief lull between the lunch and afternoon rushes. She approached our table with the determined stride of someone who had a job to do and limited time to do it.

"I need to take June Spenser's statement," she said without preamble. "Is she still here?"

"She just left, but she was planning to come talk to you anyway," I said. "She has information about private tours she gave Diana over the past month."

Denise made a note in her small book. "Good. We're starting to get a clearer picture of what Diana was doing here."

"Any updates on the investigation?" Kashvi asked hopefully.

"Still working through the evidence," Denise said, which was her standard non-answer. "I'll catch up with June at her office, then head back to the station to update the case files. Talk to the fed."

"What about Jake Webb?" I asked. "Or his father?"

"Jake came in yesterday to give his statement," Denise said, checking her watch. "Nothing earth-shattering, but he's cooperating."

After Denise left, Kashvi and I found ourselves alone at the counter as the afternoon quiet settled over us—only two booths were occupied. Even Lissa and Will had retreated to the back to help with prep work for the dinner shift.

"This is getting complicated," Kashvi said, reviewing her notes. "We've got Jake Webb and David Sterling with family motives, Emily with financial desperation, Bernie with tax problems, Pearl with accounting irregularities, and potentially several other business owners with secrets worth protecting."

"Too many suspects," I agreed, wiping down the already clean counter. "In mystery novels, that usually means the real killer is hiding in plain sight."

"Or it means we're overthinking this and the answer is simpler than we realize."

My phone buzzed with a text message from an unknown number: *Found something that might help. Can we meet somewhere private? It's about my father and Diana. - Jake*

I showed the message to Kashvi, who immediately looked concerned.

"That's pretty vague," she said. "And meeting somewhere private sounds potentially dangerous."

"But what if he really has found evidence that could solve this case?"

Kashvi gave me a hard stare. "Then maybe he should take it to the police instead of amateur investigators."

I texted back: *What kind of something? Where do you want to meet?*

Jake's response came quickly: *Old mining road off service road 12, where dad's truck was. I found something near the campsite that the police missed.*

Kashvi and I looked at each other, both clearly thinking the same things. No, too dangerous, and but it might solve the case.

"That's really isolated," she said. "If this is a trap, no one would hear us scream."

"But if it's genuine evidence, it could be the key to solving Diana's murder and clearing Cassidey of any suspicion."

"We can't go alone," Kashvi said firmly. "If we're going to do this, we need backup."

I thought about calling George or Denise, but something held me back. Maybe it was the protective instinct that made me want to make sure this was legitimate before potentially getting Jake in trouble with the police.

"What if we call Jet?" I suggested. "Let's make sure this is real evidence before we waste police time. He knows the area, and three of us together would be safer than going alone."

"And if Jake is the killer trying to lure us into a trap?"

"Then at least we'll have a witness," I said, though the words felt hollow even to me.

Kashvi was already reaching for her phone. "I'm calling Jet. And I'm bringing pepper spray."

## 28

J et arrived at the diner twenty minutes later, looking like he'd run the entire way from his last tour drop-off. His usually neat appearance was windblown, and he had that focused energy that meant he was ready for whatever adventure we were about to embark on.

"Okay," he said, settling into our booth and accepting the coffee I'd poured for him, "tell me everything. Kashvi's text just said we might have found a break in the case and needed backup for a potentially dangerous meeting."

I filled him in on Jake's message and our morning revelations about Diana's forensic accounting work. Jet listened with the same concentration that made him such a good tour guide—taking in every detail, so when people had questions, he could answer with some useful facts.

"So let me get this straight," he said when I finished. "Diana was investigating financial irregularities in multiple Nueva Vida businesses. Someone figured out what she was really doing and killed her to stop the investigation. Now Jake Webb, whose father is missing and who's been acting suspicious, wants to meet us in an isolated location to share mysterious evidence."

"That's about the size of it," Kashvi said. She didn't seem worried about it at all.

Jet tipped his head questioning the logic. "And we're considering going instead of telling the cops who are trained to deal with this kind of situation because...?"

"Because if Jake really has found evidence that could solve this case, it might be the key to protecting Cassidey and getting justice for Diana," I said.

"And because we're apparently addicted to putting ourselves in dangerous situations," Kashvi added with a rueful smile.

Jet pulled out his phone and showed us a map of the area around service road 12. "If we're going to do this, we should at least be smart about it. This mining road is pretty isolated, but there are several access points. We could approach from different directions, keep communication open, have an escape plan."

"You think it's a trap?" I asked "I think Jake Webb has been lying about his relationship with Diana, his father's been missing since she was killed, and now he wants to meet us somewhere the police won't interfere. That could be innocent, or it could be very bad news for us."

"But?" Kashvi prompted.

"But I also think Diana was killed by someone who's still out there," I said. "We still aren't certain about our theories. It's possible someone we interact with every day. And if Jake has information that could identify the real killer, we might be the only ones in a position to get it. And if he doesn't, I'd prefer not to waste police time."

As we discussed logistics, my phone rang. I didn't recognize the number, but the voice was familiar—Betty from the police station reception desk.

"Eliza?" she said, her voice hushed like she was trying not to be overheard. "I probably shouldn't be calling you, but I thought you should know what I overheard Detective Kramer telling that fed."

I gestured for Jet and Kashvi to stop talking. "What kind of thing, Betty?"

"They've confirmed it's definitely six businesses involved in some kind of financial scheme. Diana had documented everything. That fed lady seemed real excited about it, said they'd have enough evidence to make arrests soon."

My stomach dropped. "Do you know which businesses?"

"That's just it—Detective Kramer was about to give her the list when Detective Collett came back and they all went into his office and closed the door. But I heard him say he'd have the full list typed up within the hour." Betty's voice got even quieter. "I could try to get you a copy when it's ready, if you want."

"Betty, that could get you in serious trouble." I didn't want her to lose her job.

"Honey, I've been working here for twenty-three years. I know how to make copies without anyone noticing. Besides, these are our neighbors we're talking about. People have a right to know if there's a murderer running around town."

After Betty hung up, I shared her update with Kashvi and Jet.

"So now we potentially have six businesses involved in coordinated financial crimes," Jet said. "That's a lot of people with motive for murder."

"And a lot of people who might want to stop us from investigating," Kashvi added.

"Which brings us back to the question of whether we

should meet with Jake," I said. "If he has evidence about this conspiracy, it could be crucial. But if he's part of it, we could be walking into a trap."

"There's one way to find out," Jet said, checking his watch. "But we do this smart. I'll take my van and approach from the north trail. You two take your car and come from the main road. We stay in phone contact the whole time and have clear exit strategies."

"And if it goes wrong?" Kashvi asked as she checked her phone battery.

He shrugged like there was only one option. "Then we run like hell and hope we can get to our vehicles before whoever's trying to hurt us catches up."

It wasn't the most reassuring plan, but it was better than going in blind.

TWENTY MINUTES LATER, I was driving up service road 12 with Kashvi beside me, following Jet's detailed directions while staying connected to him via speakerphone. His voice crackled and cut out through my car's speakers as he navigated the more challenging northern approach in his tour van.

"I'm about five minutes out from my position," Jet's voice reported. "How are you two doing?"

"Road's getting rougher, but we're managing," I said, navigating around a particularly large pothole. "Any sign of other vehicles?"

"Nothing suspicious so far. I can see the general area where we're supposed to meet from up here. No movement yet."

We reached our designated parking spot—a small turnout hidden behind a screen of pine trees that would conceal my car from casual observation. From here, we could see the area where David Sterling's truck had been found, as well as the general location where Jake had asked us to meet.

"We're in position," I reported to Jet. "Can you see the meeting spot from where you are?"

"Good view of the whole area," his voice confirmed through the speaker. "Still no sign of anyone."

"Jake's text said he'd be here at four," I said, checking my watch. "We're fifteen minutes early."

"Good. Gives us time to observe the area and make sure this isn't an ambush."

We settled in to wait, each of us scanning different sections of the landscape for any sign of movement or potential threats. The afternoon sun slanted through the trees, creating a peaceful scene that belied the tension we all felt.

"There," Kashvi said quietly, pointing toward a trail that wound down from the higher elevations. "Someone's coming."

Through the binoculars, I could see a figure moving carefully down the trail, occasionally stopping to look around as if checking for followers. As the person got closer, I could make out Jake Webb's distinctive gait and dark hair.

"It's him," I said. "And he appears to be alone."

"Appears being the key word," Jet said. "Let's give it a few more minutes to see if anyone else shows up."

But as the minutes passed, it became clear that Jake was indeed alone. He reached the designated meeting spot—a small clearing near where his father's truck had been found from Vic's description—and stood there looking around nervously.

"Decision time," Kashvi said. "Do we go down there, or do we call this off?"

I thought about Cassidey, about Diana Whitfield, about all the secrets that seemed to be poisoning our small community.

"We go," I said. "But we stay together, we stay alert, and at the first sign of trouble, we run."

s we watched Jake's approach, my phone buzzed with a text from Betty: *Got the list! Six businesses confirmed: Emily's gift shop, Pearl's bakery, Bernie's burger place, Alistair's Dunes Cafe, Automotive Excellence (Tom Morrison's garage), and Artisan's Corner (Linda Chen's pottery studio). That fed says some are worse than others. Will try to find out more.*

I showed the text to Kashvi, who immediately pulled out her notebook to jot down the names.

"Tom Morrison," she said thoughtfully. "I don't know him well, but he's been running that garage for about five years. Always seems to have expensive cars in for custom work. Didn't we talk to his mother? David's neighbor?"

"That's right. And Linda Chen just opened Artisan's Corner last year," I added. "She imports pottery and jewelry from various countries. I always wondered how she could afford such an upscale location so quickly."

"Decision time," Jet's voice came through the speaker. "Do we go down there, or do we call this off?"

I thought again about Cassidey, about Diana Whitfield,

about all the secrets that seemed to be poisoning our small community. And now we had confirmation that six local businesses were involved in financial crimes serious enough to get the attention of the authorities—any of whom might have been desperate enough to kill Diana to protect their secrets.

"We go," I said. "But we stay together, we stay alert, and at the first sign of trouble, we run."

"Roger that," Jet said, and I had to suppress a smile at how professional he sounded. "I'm heading down to the meeting point now. You two give me a two-minute head start, then approach from your direction."

As we made our way down the trail toward Jake, I couldn't help but feel like we were approaching a moment of truth. Either Jake Webb was a scared young man trying to help find his missing father, or we were walking straight into a trap.

The trail was steeper than it had looked from above, and by the time we reached the clearing, I was slightly out of breath. Jake was standing near a large boulder, holding what looked like a plastic evidence bag containing some kind of papers.

"Thank you for coming," he said as we approached. His voice was shaky, and he kept glancing around like he expected someone to jump out of the trees.

"What did you find?" Jet asked, arriving from his approach trail at almost the same moment we did.

Jake held up the plastic bag. "These were hidden under a loose rock near where my dad's truck was parked. I think he left them for me to find."

Through the clear plastic, I could see what looked like handwritten notes and some kind of official documents. My heart started to race. Was the answer in that bag?

"What do they say?" Kashvi asked as she leaned close to the bag.

"It's my dad's handwriting," Jake said, his voice getting stronger. "He wrote that Diana Whitfield wasn't just investigating businesses randomly. She was being paid by someone specific to gather evidence about financial crimes in Nueva Vida."

"Paid by whom?" I asked. I wanted to hear his lies. Diana was on assignment from her boss, not taking money to investigate, but I'm sure Jake didn't know we had those details.

"That's the thing—my dad found out who hired her," Jake said. He looked at the bag and shook his head like he couldn't believe the contents. "It's someone we all know. Someone who's been using the investigation to eliminate their competition while protecting their own illegal activities."

Jake's hands were shaking as he held the bag. "According to these notes, Diana discovered that one of the businesses she was investigating was actually money laundering for criminal organizations."

"Money laundering?" Jet repeated. "In Nueva Vida?"

Jake held out the bag of documents, not to hand it over, but like its existence was proof. "That's what my dad wrote. Diana found evidence that someone was using their legitimate business to clean money from drug trafficking and other criminal activities. When she threatened to expose them, they killed her."

"And your father went into hiding because he figured out who it was?" I asked. "He should have gone to the police." Maybe he couldn't report what he found because he had his own secrets to protect?

Jake nodded. "He was afraid they'd kill him too if they

knew he had this information. So he hid his truck and went into the wilderness until he could figure out what to do."

"Jake," Kashvi said gently, "why didn't your father just take this to the police?"

Jake's expression darkened. "Because according to his notes, the person running the money laundering operation has connections to law enforcement. Dad wasn't sure who he could trust."

The implications of that statement hung in the air like a storm cloud. If someone involved in serious criminal activity had connections to the police, it would explain how Diana's cover had been blown and why her killer hadn't been caught. And under the old sheriff, the Nueva Vida police department was corrupt, so it almost made sense.

"Do the notes say who it is?" I asked.

Jake looked around nervously before answering. "Tom Morrison. The guy who owns Automotive Excellence. Dad wrote that Morrison's been using his garage to launder money from a drug trafficking operation based in Santa Fe. Diana had proof, and when she confronted him about it, he killed her."

Tom Morrison. I tried to think of what I knew about him. He'd moved to Nueva Vida about five years ago and opened his garage, specializing in custom car work and restorations. He always seemed to have expensive vehicles in his shop, and he'd made some costly upgrades to his building recently.

"This is way beyond what the other businesses were doing," Jet said. "Tax evasion and minor fraud are one thing, but money laundering for drug traffickers..."

"That's a federal crime with serious prison time," I finished. "Definitely worth killing to protect. It's weird that David found this proof and yet Sarah has no clue about it."

"Or she just didn't mention it," Kashvi said. "Jake, we need to take this to the police immediately. This is evidence of murder."

"But what if Morrison has connections in the police department?" Jake asked. "What if we're just warning him that we know?"

It was a valid concern. If Tom Morrison really did have law enforcement connections, going to the wrong person could be dangerous for all of us.

"We take it to George," I said finally. "Whatever issues we might have with the investigation, I trust him to handle this properly."

"Are you sure?" Jake asked.

"I'm sure," I said, though I hoped I wasn't making a mistake. "George Kramer is a good cop, and he wants to solve Diana's murder as much as we do."

As we prepared to leave the clearing, Jake suddenly stopped and looked back at the spot where his father's truck had been found.

"There's something else," he said. "According to Dad's notes, Tom Morrison isn't working alone. He has a partner in the money laundering operation. Someone else in town who's been helping him clean the drug money."

"Who?" I asked, though I wasn't sure I wanted to know the answer.

"Dad wasn't sure, but he suspected it was someone with access to financial records. Someone who could help make the transactions look legitimate."

"George will find the answers," I said. "Give me the bag and we'll take care of it."

Jake tossed the evidence to me and stepped back. "I'm going to keep looking for my dad." He turned and ran down the path before I could argue that he needed to meet George.

The afternoon sun was getting lower, casting longer shadows through the trees. As we made our way back to our vehicles, I couldn't shake the feeling that we'd opened a door to something much darker than we'd expected.

Nueva Vida's charm was its simplicity, its sense of community, its distance from the kinds of serious crimes that plagued bigger cities. But now it seemed like our little town had been harboring secrets that went far beyond tax evasion and petty fraud

"Let's get this to George as quickly as possible," I said as we reached our cars. "The sooner Tom Morrison is arrested, the safer everyone will be."

## 30

W e met back at the diner an hour later, the evidence bag Jake had found sitting on the table between us like an unexploded bomb. I'd called George from the car, and he was on his way with Sarah Martinez to examine what Jake's father had hidden. We'd agreed to ignore our curiosity and not open the bag without the authorities.

The diner was quiet in the early evening lull between late lunch and early dinner, with only Woody Howell nursing a cup of coffee at the counter and reading his newspaper. Jacquie was prepping for the evening shift in the kitchen, and the familiar sounds of chopping and sizzling provided a comforting backdrop to our tense conversation.

"I still can't believe Tom Morrison is involved in money laundering," Kashvi said, shaking her head. "He serviced my car last week. I thought he was a regular guy. I mean, a bit less chatty than I like, but still..."

"That's probably the point," Jet said. "Who would suspect a small-town mechanic of cleaning drug money?

And it was nice for Conrad's Cars to have a bit of competition."

Jake had joined us shortly after we arrived, apparently realizing he wouldn't be able to find his dad without help. He sat across from us, looking more relaxed than he'd been on the mining trail. Handing us his father's evidence seemed to have lifted a weight from his shoulders.

"My dad's always been good at reading people," he said. "If he says Morrison is dangerous, I believe him."

I guess a good thing coming from Diana's murder was it gave David and Jake an opening to heal the rift between them. I hoped they would try; families were too valuable to toss them away over a disagreement

The door chimed, and George walked in with Sarah Martinez, both of them wearing the serious expressions of law enforcement officers about to examine crucial evidence.

"Jake," George said, settling into our booth, "I appreciate you bringing this to us. Can you walk us through exactly how you found these documents?"

Jake repeated his story about searching the area near his father's abandoned truck and finding the plastic bag hidden under a loose rock. Sarah took careful notes while George examined the documents without removing them from the evidence bag.

"This handwriting—you're certain it's your father's?" George asked.

"Absolutely. I've seen his writing my whole life." Jake squirmed a bit as he spoke, not liking the fact that George didn't simply believe him.

"And he specifically names Tom Morrison as the person running a money laundering operation?"

Sarah took the bag and tried to read through the plastic. She unzipped the top and gently removed the papers. The writing was crowded and hard to read upside down. I was regretting our decision to leave the bag sealed. Now it was in professional hands, we'd never know what David wrote.

Jake sat up straight and answered George, keeping his eyes on Sarah. "Yes, sir. Says Diana had proof and that Morrison killed her when she threatened to expose him."

George and Sarah exchanged meaningful glances. I wanted desperately to ask what she'd read but I kept my lips pressed together to stop the words just popping out. Kashvi was doing the same but Jet leaned back in the booth as casual as if he was waiting for his coffee.

"We'll need to verify this information," Sarah said carefully, "but if it's accurate, it explains a lot about Diana's murder. I'll get a warrant to search your father's belongings. Get a separate writing sample for comparison."

Jake squirmed again, and I expected him to object, or offer to let them in without a warrant, but he didn't speak.

"What happens now?" I asked.

"Now we investigate Tom Morrison very carefully," George said. "If he's really involved in money laundering for drug traffickers, we need to handle this properly to avoid tipping him off."

"In the meantime," Sarah added, "I should probably update you on our investigation into the other businesses Diana was looking at. We've completed our review of the financial irregularities."

"These are civilians," George said, putting his hand on her notebook. He pointedly looked at Jake, and I took that to mean he trusted us but not him.

"I should go anyway," Jake said. "Thanks for believing me. Maybe I can find Dad now and he'll be safe to come out of hiding." He slid out of the booth and out the door.

Sarah pulled out a folder and consulted her notes. "If we

want their help, we can't just let them go in blind. I'll take the heat if something goes wrong."

George removed his hand from her notebook and carefully placed the sheets back in the original container and into an evidence bag. "Fine. I wish you'd all stay out of the case, but I know that's not going to happen.

Sarah smiled at his words, not in an 'I won' way, but more like she was encouraged by his flexibility.

"Emily Stonehouse will face civil penalties for her investment scheme, but we're recommending against criminal charges given her cooperation and the relatively small amounts involved." She flipped a page. "Pearl Sargent and Bernie Castro will receive fines for tax reporting issues, but again, nothing criminal, and we'll offer a payment plan. Our job isn't to shut down small businesses, just to make sure there's a level playing field."

"What about Alistair McKay?" Kashvi asked. "He's going to have a conniption no matter what."

"Mr. McKay's situation is a bit more complicated," Sarah said with what might have been the ghost of a smile. "And not just because he's so defensive. He's been significantly underreporting his income and claiming false business expenses. He'll face substantial fines and will need to pay back taxes with interest."

As Kashvi said, it wouldn't matter if the fine was a hundred dollars—Alistair would blow up the impact like it was a life sentence. "And Linda Chen?" I asked, remembering the sixth name on Betty's list.

"Ms. Chen has been importing artwork without properly declaring its value to customs. She'll face penalties from both the IRS and customs enforcement, but nothing that would warrant arrest. I'm pretty sure she was about to cross the line, but we caught her in time."

"So out of the six businesses, only Tom Morrison was involved in serious criminal activity?" Jet asked.

I was relieved beyond just not being on the list. I kept my books clean, and so did Kashvi, so we weren't under scrutiny. It sounded like June was in the same boat as us, so Jet's job was safe. Even more, it was good to know that most of our neighbors and friends weren't hardened criminals, just people who'd made poor financial decisions under pressure.

"If Jake's father's information is correct, yes," George said. "The others were guilty of various forms of tax evasion or minor fraud, but Morrison was using his legitimate business to clean money from major criminal organizations."

"George," I said, "when you arrest Morrison, what happens to the other business owners?"

"They'll receive their penalties through the proper legal channels," he said. "Right now they don't know, so keep it to yourselves. It will take a few days for the notices to go out."

George's phone buzzed with what looked like an urgent message. He read it and immediately stood up.

"We need to go," he said to Sarah. "Tom Morrison just closed his garage unexpectedly and hasn't been seen since this afternoon."

"The news is out I guess," Sarah said.

"Looks like it," George said. "Someone might have tipped him off that we were getting close."

"How would anyone know?" I asked. Did Betty broadcast it? Or just tell Martha?

George's expression was grim. "That's what we need to find out. If Morrison really does have connections in law enforcement, we might have a leak in the department. Or it could be his money laundering client. There's no sign of any partner."

After George and Sarah left to coordinate the search for

Tom Morrison, we sat in the quiet diner processing what we'd learned.

"At least we know who killed Diana," Jet said. "I mean, most likely, right? Tom has the clearer motive."

"If Tom Morrison is really the killer," Kashvi said. "We're taking Jake's father's word for it, but we haven't actually verified any of this independently. Even the handwriting needs to be checked."

"You think Jake's lying?" I asked. I wasn't fully convinced, but I couldn't put my mental finger on why I didn't trust him.

"I think Jake believes what he told us," Kashvi said, sitting forward and picking up the menu. "But what if his father was wrong? What if Tom Morrison is just someone who made a really bad decision? The real killer could still be out there."

It was a sobering thought. We'd been so relieved to have a clear answer that we might not have questioned it as carefully as we should have. Lissa took our orders and refilled our drinks. We were all hungry and a bit worn out from the tangles of information.

"There's only one way to find out," I said. "We wait to see if the police find evidence to support David Sterling's accusations."

"And in the meantime?" Jet asked.

"In the meantime, we go back to our normal lives and hope that Tom Morrison really was Diana's killer. Because if he wasn't..."

I didn't finish the sentence, but we all understood the implication. If Tom Morrison wasn't the murderer, then Diana's real killer was still in Nueva Vida, probably watching our investigation and waiting for the right moment to strike again.

As if to underscore my fears, my phone buzzed with another text from an unknown number: *Tom Morrison didn't kill Diana Whitfield. Stop investigating before you get hurt.*

I showed the message to the others, and I saw my own fear reflected in their faces.

"Someone really doesn't want us to discover the truth," Kashvi said quietly.

"The question is," Jet said, "are we getting close to the real killer, or are we being led away from them? The text might be from Tom trying to distract us while he flees."

Lissa delivered our burgers and fries as Jet's words sunk in. The aroma of the beef and hot crispy potatoes did nothing to alleviate my worries, and everything to remind me I was starving.

## 31

The next morning brought news that Tom Morrison had been found and arrested at a truck stop outside Albuquerque, trying to board a bus to Mexico. His garage had been searched, revealing sophisticated money laundering records documenting transactions totaling over two million dollars in the past three months. I never understood why criminals kept the proof of their crimes on hand.

I was reading about it in the Nueva Vida Record and wondering why George hadn't given me a heads-up while enjoying my second cup of coffee. The buzz of normal breakfast service, accompanied by the aromas of bacon, pancake batter, and freshly brewed coffee, took away the sting of being left out. I wasn't needed to help so I relaxed—it wouldn't be long before I as running around keeping diners happy.

My mind was occupied with the coming week's menu, which would include the satay with rice and salad, when Alistair McKay burst through the diner door like a theatrical hurricane. His usual dramatic flair was amplified by what appeared to be genuine outrage, and every customer in the place turned to watch his entrance—most of them with expressions of amusement. Like he was the floor show and they were about to be highly entertained.

"You!" he declared, pointing directly at me from the center of the dining room. "This is all your fault!"

"Good morning to you too, Alistair," I said, setting down my newspaper with deliberate calm. "Coffee?"

"Don't you dare offer me coffee like we're friends!" he proclaimed, his voice carrying to every corner of the diner. "I just got off the phone with some federal agent who informed me that I owe the government nearly fifty thousand dollars in back taxes and penalties!"

Several customers shifted uncomfortably in their seats, clearly torn between the entertainment value of Alistair's performance and the awkwardness of witnessing someone's financial humiliation. I figured Alistair either didn't care that he was proclaiming his misdeeds or hadn't realized.

"Alistair," I said gently, "the government discovered your tax issues through their own investigation. I had nothing to do with that."

"Nothing to do with it?" He gestured wildly, his voice reaching new theatrical heights. "You and your little detective club have been running around town asking questions, stirring up trouble, encouraging people to confess to crimes they didn't even know they'd committed!"

"We were trying to solve a murder," Anthone said, appearing from the kitchen with four plates of waffles and bacon for a booth full of customers. "Which, I might point out, we helped do."

"By ruining innocent people's lives!" Alistair shot back. "Emily Stonehouse is facing bankruptcy! Bernie Castro might lose his restaurant! Pearl Sargent is so stressed she's had to close the bakery for a week!"

I felt a pang of guilt. While I was glad Diana's killer had been caught, I hadn't fully considered the collateral damage our investigation might cause to people who were guilty of nothing more than poor financial judgment.

It also wasn't his place to reveal other people's problems. He'd make even more enemies with this display.

"Do they know you're shouting their business to all and sundry, Alistair?" I asked, sipping from my half-empty cup.

"It's common knowledge," he shouted. "Or it will be soon. You'll have more than me angry at you."

That was too much. "I wish you wouldn't keep coming here to entertain my diners with your histrionics."

"Well, the woman's dead!" he declared, throwing his arms wide. "If you hadn't stirred everything up, maybe the government would have forgotten all about her investigation!"

"Or maybe Tom Morrison would have killed someone else to keep his money laundering operation secret," Cassidey said. She'd joined Anthone at the counter. "You don't know how hard it is to say no to a gang leader. Or, maybe you do." Her eyes gleamed with mischief. "Rumor has it that Mr. Morrison had a partner."

"Well, you certainly know the ins and outs of gangs," Alistair said, pointing his finger at her.

"That's enough!" Woody stood from his booth where he'd been enjoying the show. "It's bad enough you do this to Eliza, but she's an adult and able to hold her own. That child is not your target. Time to leave, Alistair, and if I see you in this diner again, I'll drag you out by your ear."

That was quite a shock. Woody did have his protective

side, but I'd never seen him go after anyone. I guess we weren't Cassidey's only family.

Alistair huffed his annoyance, as if that would scare anyone off. He did drop his accusing finger and turn away. "I was going anyway."

After he stormed out, everyone turned back to their food. Cassidey thanked Woody and returned to her lessons in the kitchen.

George walked through the door five minutes later. "Heard you had a visitor," he said, settling onto a counter stool.

"News travels fast," I said, pouring his coffee into a to-go cup. "How's the Morrison case developing?"

"I'm not going to tell you it's official business because I never seem to win that argument. It's better than I expected. He's decided to cooperate in exchange for a reduced sentence. Turns out he was just the local operation—there's a much larger network we're now investigating, out of Albuquerque. I'm worried that our local hooligans are going to be drawn in."

I hoped not, but until the cops and the community came to an agreement on how to deal with what was right now a group of misbehaving kids that called itself a gang, the possibility remained of them turning into real criminals.

"What about the partner?" I asked. "Even Alistair heard that rumor."

George shook his head. "I think Jake is talking to anyone who'll listen in the hopes he can find David. The thing is, Morrison claims he was working alone here in Nueva Vida, just providing services to the larger organization. But we're still investigating."

"What about David Sterling?" I asked. "Is he safe to come out of hiding now?"

"We're working on locating him to let him know Morrison's been arrested. Jake's been helpful in narrowing down where his father might be camping, but so far, nothing."

I poured myself a fresh cup of coffee and stood at the counter across from George. "So Diana's murder is solved, the money laundering operation is shut down, and the tax evaders are facing appropriate penalties. Case closed?"

"We can't close the case on Diana's murder," George said. "Morrison is denying any involvement. The larger investigation into the money laundering network will continue for months. So maybe he'll break after more interrogation."

I wouldn't feel settled until they were sure they'd arrested the killer. It seemed weird that Tom would deny the murder when he was making a deal. "And Jake Webb? Is he in any trouble for not coming forward sooner with his father's information?"

George added sugar to his coffee. "As far as I can tell, Jake's a victim in all this, not a perpetrator. He was scared and trying to protect his father. Under the circumstances, his actions were understandable. Let's remember, Diana was his step-mother."

After George left to continue his work on the larger investigation, with a quick reminder of our date. I expected to feel a sense of closure, but I worried that, case solved or not, Nueva Vida was gaining the wrong kind of attention. The next few weeks of the festival season might help us put the crimes into the past, but there was no guarantee the criminals would cooperate.

I pushed the thought aside and focused on the familiar comfort of running my diner. Whatever doubts lingered would have to wait. Nueva Vida needed time to heal, and I needed to focus on taking care of my community, my employees, and my customers.

## 32

Three days after Tom Morrison's arrest, I found myself back in the familiar comfort of Kashvi's bookstore back room, staring at our murder board with a growing sense of unease. Despite all the evidence against Morrison, something kept nagging at me about Diana Whitfield's death. Why did he continue to insist he was innocent of murder?

"I still don't understand the timeline," I said, pointing to our carefully constructed sequence of events. "Morrison was supposedly cleaning money for drug traffickers. Killing a federal investigator would bring attention, so wouldn't it be done more... discreetly? Doing it at a public fair seems too showy."

Jet, who was reading over his notes at the table, looked up and took a swig of his coffee. "Plus, the whole peanut oil thing seems really complicated for a panicked killer. If Morrison wanted Diana dead, wouldn't he have just... I don't know, shot her or something more direct? It does seem odd that he'd know about her allergy."

"Exactly," Kashvi said, making notes in her notebook.

"Poisoning someone with peanut oil at a public fair requires intimate knowledge of their allergy, and the opportunity to contaminate their food without being seen. Getting the oil is the easiest part—no one would remember selling such a common item. The way she was killed is not the work of a desperate money launderer—that's personal."

The back room door opened, and Cassidey walked in carrying a tray of coffee and sandwiches from the diner. I'd invited her to join what I'd thought would be our post-case analysis partly because she'd been such a crucial witness, and partly because I wanted her to feel like a full member of our little community. Right now it felt like we were restarting from step one, not wrapping it up.

"Thought you might be hungry," she said, setting the tray on Kashvi's work table. "It's almost dinnertime, and thinking takes energy."

"You figured right," I said, accepting a sandwich gratefully. "We're having trouble believing that Tom Morrison really killed Diana."

Cassidey settled into the remaining chair and studied our murder board with the careful attention of someone who'd learned to read situations quickly for survival.

"Wait, can I ask something?" she said, tilting her head like she was working through a puzzle. "This Morrison guy —was he even at the fair when that lady died?"

The question hit us like a shot of hot sauce on the tongue. We'd been so focused on Morrison's money laundering operation that we'd never actually verified his whereabouts during the crucial time period.

"Oh my God," Kashvi said, flipping through her notes frantically. "I don't think we ever established that. Do any of us remember seeing him at the fair?"

I tried to think back to that chaotic day. "I remember

seeing most of the regular business owners, but Morrison...
I'm not sure I saw him at all."

"His garage doesn't do food service," Jet pointed out. "He
wouldn't have had a booth at the fair."

"But he could have attended as a customer," I said,
though even as I said it, Tom Morrison didn't strike me as
the type to wander around sampling food at community
events. I didn't know how money laundering operations
worked, but I always figured it was the kind work you
couldn't leave, like not watching a pan of caramel on the
stove. Too many things could go wrong fast.

Cassidey was still staring at the murder board, chewing
on her bottom lip the way she did when she was concentrating hard. "Okay, but here's another thing that's bugging
me," she said. "If Morrison killed Diana to protect his
money stuff, how would Jake's dad even know about it? Like,
what's the connection?"

Another excellent point. We'd accepted Jake's story
about his father discovering Morrison's guilt without questioning how David would have come by that information.

"And also," Cassidey continued, getting more animated
as she worked through the logic, "doesn't it seem super
convenient that Jake found those papers right when we
needed someone to blame who wasn't him or his dad? I
mean, come on."

"Cassidey, what are you suggesting?" I wanted to let her
take it to the end.

"If Jake Webb killed Diana, things kind of make sense.
When you guys started getting too close to figuring it out, he
decided to pin it on Morrison instead. I'm not sure why he
picked him, though." She looked around at all of us. "Is that
totally crazy?"

"Not crazy at all," Kashvi said slowly. "But why would

Jake want to kill Diana? She wasn't investigating him or David. Neither of them owns a business."

"Money?" Cassidey said, like it was obvious. "I mean, isn't it always about money? Diana was like his stepmom or whatever, right?"

"Ex-stepmother," I corrected. "David and Diana were divorced."

"But Jake might not have known all the details about the divorce and stuff," Cassidey said, warming to her theory. "What if he thought he was gonna inherit from her when she died? Because all her money came from the divorce settlement? What if she came here to tell him and his dad that she was changing her will or something?"

The pieces started falling into place with horrible clarity, and I found myself amazed at how quickly Cassidey had seen through Jake's deception. Her insight was remarkable for someone so young—though I supposed surviving on the streets had taught her to read people and situations better than most adults. And living in a shelter put her in contact with people in desperate situations.

"Oh, dear," I said. "What if David isn't hiding from Tom Morrison? What if he's hiding from his own son?"

"And what if those papers Jake 'found' were totally fake?" Cassidey finished, looking pleased with herself for working it all out.

We all stared at the murder board, seeing the case from a completely different angle. Jake Webb had been present at the fair—he could have bought the peanut oil at Valdez's— knew about Diana's allergy from family history, and had been lying about his relationship with her from the beginning.

"We need to call George," I said, reaching for my phone.

"Wait," Cassidey said, suddenly looking younger and

more worried. "Do you think he'll believe you? I mean, that Sarah lady is taking Mr. Morrison into custody, and our cops seem convinced he's the killer too."

Looking at her earnest face, I was struck by the contradiction of someone so young having such mature insights about criminal behavior. Cassidey had mentioned once that she'd thought about becoming a private investigator after watching us solve our first case.

"So what do you suggest we do?" Kashvi asked.

"I don't know—you guys are the investigators. I just want you safe."

"We gather more evidence before we make any accusations," I said. "But we do it very, very carefully and quickly."

As if summoned by our conversation, my phone buzzed with a text message from Jake: *Need to talk to you about my father. Can you meet me at the diner in 30? I have new information about Morrison's partner.*

I showed the message to the others, and I saw my own fear reflected in their faces. The diner was closed, and the crew would have cleaned up and left by then.

"He knows," Cassidey said quietly. "Somehow, he knows we've figured it out. Is this place bugged?"

"I don't think so, and he's never been in the back room to do it." Kashvi looked under the table as she talked to check for a listening device.

"The question is," Jet said, "do we meet with him and try to get a confession, or do we call George and let the police handle it?"

I thought about Diana Whitfield, about Cassidey's safety, about all the lies Jake had told us while we'd tried to help him. I didn't have a convenient deathly allergy, so if he wanted me gone, it would be loud and messy.

"We call George," I said. "But first, we make sure we have

somewhere more controllable to go. Because if Jake Webb really is a killer, none of us are safe until he's behind bars."

As I dialed George's number, I couldn't help but think about how wrong we'd been about Jake. We'd seen him as a scared young man trying to help his father, when in reality he was a cold-blooded killer who'd murdered his step-mother for money and then manipulated our investigation to frame an innocent man.

## 33

George arrived at the bookstore within two minutes of my call, accompanied by Denise and two uniformed officers. We'd moved to the main part of the store because none of us needed the lecture that would come when any of them saw the murder board.

"You think Jake killed Diana and framed Tom Morrison?" George asked, with a blink of shock after I filled him in.

"There's nothing to put Morrison at the fair," I said. "And Jake had motive, means, and opportunity."

"Plus he's been lying to us from the beginning," Kashvi added. "About knowing Diana, about his relationship with his father, probably about those papers he supposedly found. I still can't believe it took us so long to make the connections."

George was quiet for a long moment, processing our theory. "It's possible," he said finally. "Morrison's been maintaining his innocence about the murder, even though he's confessed to the money laundering. Says he'd never heard of Diana Whitfield."

"What about Jake's text asking to meet at the diner?" Cassidey asked, fidgeting with nerves but clearly determined to be part of the conversation.

"We're going to set up surveillance," Denise said. "If Jake really is the killer and he thinks you're getting too close to the truth, this could be his attempt to eliminate witnesses."

"I'm not using Eliza as bait," George said firmly. "And the diner has too many sharp potential weapons."

I thought of all the kitchen knives and agreed. "Good point," I said. "I can text Jake back and suggest we meet somewhere else. Somewhere the police can control the situation. Not that I'll say those words."

Fifteen minutes later—and ten minutes before the deadline—we had a plan. I would text Jake to suggest meeting at the park near the fairgrounds instead of the diner, claiming I wanted to talk somewhere private and the diner might not be secure. Police would be positioned throughout the area, and I would wear a wire to record any confession. And we'd convinced Cassidey to head home until the danger had passed.

"I don't like this," Jet said as Denise fitted me with the recording equipment. "If Jake really is a killer, you're putting yourself in serious danger."

"I'll be surrounded by police," I said, trying to sound more confident than I felt. "And if we can get him to confess, we'll have justice for Diana and closure for the community."

"Just be careful," Kashvi said. "Don't try to be a hero. Get him talking and let the police handle the rest."

As the sun set, I made my way to the park, hyperaware of the police officers hidden in various positions around the area. I kept reminding myself that they were experts at arresting people, and I knew they were there which should feel comforting, but didn't.

I saw Jake as I turned a corner past a giant yucca. He'd arrived early, taking a position on a bench and turning his head to keep every angle in sight. I didn't expect that level of vigilance. Were we wrong? Wouldn't a killer be calm and icy?

"Thanks for meeting me," he said as I approached. "I wasn't sure you'd come."

"You said you had new information about Morrison's partner," I said, sitting down carefully beside him.

"Actually," Jake said, his voice taking on a different, sharper tone, "I wanted to talk to you about your investigation. I think you've been asking too many questions."

"What kind of questions?" I asked, trying to keep my voice steady but suddenly thankful for our observers.

"Questions about me. About my relationship with Diana. About why I lied about knowing her."

I felt my heart rate increase, but I forced myself to stay calm. "Jake, if you have something to tell me, now would be a good time. As far as we know, the case is closed."

He was quiet for a long moment, staring at his hands. "Diana Whitfield was my stepmother," he said finally. "Well, ex-stepmother. She raised me for five years when I was a kid, before my parents got divorced."

I heard George's advice in my head—get him talking and he won't be able to stop. "Why didn't you tell us that from the beginning?"

"Because I knew it would make me look guilty. And because..." He paused, struggling with something. "I can't hide it any longer. Because I did kill her."

Even though I'd been expecting it, hearing the confession come so quickly still shocked me. "Why, Jake?"

"Money," he said simply. "I was going to inherit from her when she died. My dad lost everything in the divorce, but Diana walked away with millions. I figured when she died, some of that money would come to me. It wasn't really hers, right?"

"So when she came to Nueva Vida on a job, she thought it was a good time to visit you?"

Jake's expression darkened. "She came to tell me and my father that she'd changed her will. Everything was going to charity. I was going to get nothing."

But she didn't get a chance to tell him anything, I thought. "So you killed her before she could tell you officially?" Did he think that was a legal step?

"I panicked," he said. "I'd been counting on that inheritance. I had debts, plans, a whole future mapped out based on money I thought would be mine. When Dad told me about the will change, I just... snapped."

George would need more details to make the arrest, so I needed to keep Jake talking. "How did you do it?"

"I knew about her peanut allergy from when we were a family. I brought a small bottle of peanut oil to the fair and waited for the right moment. When she was sitting alone at the picnic table, I approached her, said I wanted to talk. I touched her hand like I was begging her to listen. The oil on my fingers transferred. It only took a drop. I guess she picked up one of the samples and enough got into her."

He grinned at me, and my stomach twisted.

"And she trusted you because you were family."

"She was always trying to rebuild our relationship after she divorced my dad," Jake said bitterly. "Always reaching out, trying to be a mother figure. It made it easy to get close to her."

"What about your father? Does he know what you did?"

Please say he didn't know because if he did and covered it up...

"Dad figured it out pretty quickly. Diana told him she'd been planning to change her will, and when she died before she could tell us officially, he put the pieces together. That's why he went into hiding—he was afraid of me, and afraid that if he went to the police, they wouldn't believe him."

"And Tom Morrison?" I know it was pushing my luck, but how had he known about Tom's activities?

"I needed a scapegoat when you started getting too close to the truth. Morrison was already guilty of money laundering, so it was easy to frame him for murder too. I forged those papers and made up the story about finding them near Dad's truck."

"Why are you telling me this?" It was like a switch had been flicked. One moment he was denying everything and the next the whole story bubbled out of him."

"I can't sleep. I keep thinking about her dying." He slid his hand into his pocket and drew out a knife. "I wasn't planning on letting you tell anyone else."

"Jake," I said gently, trying to ignore the knife. He wasn't ready to use it, and I wanted more on the recording. I figured I could move fast if his attitude went from confession to murder. "Diana's will had already been changed. You killed her for nothing."

His face collapsed as he heard the words. "What do you mean?"

"She'd already filed the paperwork with her lawyer. The will was changed weeks before she came to Nueva Vida. She was coming to tell you in person as a courtesy, not to warn you before she did it."

Jake stared at me in horror as the full implications sank in. The knife clattered to the pavement. He'd murdered someone he'd once considered a mother figure for money he was never going to receive anyway. Or, did he think he'd use his inheritance to avoid prison? "So it was all for nothing?"

"I need you to stand up slowly and put your hands behind your back," George's voice came from behind us as police officers emerged from their hiding places.

George glanced at the knife and the glared at me. I guess I should have mentioned it for the tape.

Jake didn't resist as they handcuffed him. He looked broken, defeated, like someone who'd finally realized the true cost of his actions.

As the police cars disappeared into the night, I stood in the empty park feeling drained and sad. Justice had been served, but it didn't feel like a victory. A young man's greed and desperation had destroyed multiple lives, including his own.

## 34

Two days later, we were gathered in my living room, Macchiato in the corner staring at people's ankles as if she was a lion and the people were prey.

I'd ordered pastries from Pearl's bakery, trying to help give her a little business to ease the pain of her fines. Three bottles of champagne sat in ice beside the trays. The murder board in Kashvi's back room was dismantled the night George took Jake into custody. And now we could celebrate.

"So," Kashvi said, settling into her chair with a satisfied smile, "another case solved, another killer behind bars. I'd say we're getting pretty good at this amateur detective thing."

"Too good," I said, thinking about how close we'd all come to danger. "I'm hoping Nueva Vida goes back to being the quiet little town I fell in love with. Or if it must host another murder, we won't be involved."

"Though I have to admit, the tourists love hearing about our murder investigations," Jet said, holding up his champagne in salute. "My bookings are up thirty percent since the news broke about Jake Webb. June's trying to come up with enough content to launch a 'darkest secrets' tour."

Cassidey, who was curled up in the corner chair with Macchiato purring in her lap—ankle attacks forgotten for pets—looked up from the cat with a grin. "I still can't believe I was the one who figured out Jake was lying. I mean, I would never have figured that out before I helped at the fair."

"You were the one who saw what the rest of us missed," I said. "Fresh eyes, different perspective. Plus, you understand desperation and deception better than any of us, unfortunately."

"Speaking of which," Kashvi said, "how are you settling into your new permanent position?"

Cassidey's face lit up. "It's amazing. I love working at the diner, I love having my own little apartment above the hardware store, and I love being part of a community that actually cares about me. For the first time in my life, I feel like I have a real future."

"And you're completely out of the gang life?" Jet asked.

"I made a deal," she said, looking back down at the purring mass of feline in her lap. "They let me alone, and I won't help the police bust up the gang. I know I'm off the hook because I'm a kid, but you use what you have."

I felt a warm glow of satisfaction. At least one good thing had come out of all the chaos and investigation. She was still a kid despite everything. I'd signed her lease for the apartment. Anthone was working with Bernie's catering company more and more, so I had a vacancy she could fill. Her case worker dropped by to check on Cassidey but told me she had more challenging cases and Cassidey was in safe hands with us.

"Speaking of the future," Kashvi said with a mischievous

glint in her eye, "how did your dates go? And don't pretend you don't know what I'm talking about—this is a small town. Word gets around."

I felt heat rise in my cheeks. "You heard about both of them?"

"Martha at the post office saw you and Vic at the restaurant," Jet said with a grin. "And June Spenser spotted you and George at the art gallery. So spill—which one's the keeper?"

I took a large sip of champagne to buy myself time. "Well, the dinner with Vic was... educational."

"Educational how?" Cassidey asked, clearly invested in the romantic drama.

"It turns out that while Vic is wonderful in emergencies and great at casual conversation, he's absolutely terrible at formal date conversation. We spent two hours discussing fire safety regulations and the proper maintenance of emergency equipment."

"Oof," Kashvi said with sympathy. "That's rough. And really surprising."

"Not romantic at all," I agreed. "Sweet guy, but zero chemistry when we're trying to be romantic instead of just friends who occasionally get together."

"And George?" Jet prompted.

"George," I said, unable to suppress a smile, "was a complete surprise. I was expecting him to be all serious and professional, but he actually knows a lot about art. We spent three hours at the gallery talking about everything from local artists to travel destinations to books we'd read. He's funny, thoughtful, and when he's not in detective mode, he's actually quite charming."

"So George wins?" Cassidey asked hopefully.

"No one wins," I said. "Vic admitted he was a dud at

small talk. We're going on a hike. I guess we need to get more comfortable before we face another fancy dinner."

"You get to date two guys?" Cassidey asked. "Not just two of them but guys who hate each other."

"Hate is too strong a word," I said not quite believing it. "I'm not ready for commitment yet, so dating is as far as it goes."

"Plus," Jet added, "dating the lead investigator means you'll get inside information on any future murders."

"There better not be any future murders," I said firmly. "This town has had enough excitement to last several lifetimes."

We sat in comfortable silence for a few minutes, enjoying the peaceful afternoon and the satisfaction of a case well solved. Through the front windows, I could see the landscape of gentle colors and warm sunshine. My new home, back to being the safe place where I curled up with my cat and a book after a long day of feeding people.

"You know what the best part of all this is?" Cassidey said, scratching Macchiato behind the ears.

"What's that?" I asked.

"For the first time since my mom died, I feel like I have a family again. You all took care of me, protected me, trusted me, and believed in me when I didn't believe in myself." She looked down at Macchiato again. "Sorry for being kind of emo, but I had to say it."

I felt tears prick my eyes. "You are family, Cassidey. All of us are family now."

"The Nueva Vida Detective Club family," Jet said with mock solemnity.

"Please don't call it that," Kashvi said, laughing. "We sound like a bunch of kids playing dress-up. And I don't want to get better at it."

"How about the EB Eats Investigation Society?" I suggested, ignoring her objection to keep the fun going.

"Better," Cassidey said. "Though hopefully we won't need to investigate anything more serious than missing pie recipes."

"From your lips to God's ears," I said, raising my champagne. "To family, to justice, and to boring, peaceful small-town life."

"To family," the others echoed, and we clinked our glasses together in a toast to friendship, community, and the hope that Nueva Vida's murder investigation days were finally behind us.

Visitors come to a yoga retreat to recharge and reenergize not to get murdered. Eliza pokes into secrets and lies to find the real culprit before an innocent man is sent to jail.

Use the QR code to check out With A Side of Death now!

Claim your copy of Burned by BLT when you sign up for my newsletter learn how Eliza became so determined to clear her name.

~

If you enjoyed reading DEATH ON THE MENU please consider helping other readers to find the story by leaving a review.

# ALSO BY POPPY

For more books by Poppy Bridgeman

scan the QR code below.

# ABOUT POPPY BRIDGEMAN

Hi, I'm Poppy Bridgeman, the cozy mystery alter ego of Canadian author P A Wilson. Poppy was "born" because sometimes stories need a gentler touch—with a little magic, a dash of humor, and plenty of sleuthing spirit.

As Poppy, I write the *Witch of Henbane Island* series (where witches and festivals collide with mysteries), the *EB Eats Culinary Mysteries* (a small-town diner, a determined heroine, and murder on the menu), and the *Pages & Paws Bookstore Mysteries* (a Devon bookshop, two mischievous corgis, and plenty of secrets tucked between the shelves).

When I'm not tangled in my characters' escapades, I'm happily tangled in yarn—I knit, weave, and doodle in sketchbooks between writing sessions. I also love to travel, finding inspiration for charming settings, quirky characters, and suspicious strangers wherever I go.

Home base is the Vancouver area, where I juggle writing as both Poppy and P A Wilson. Whichever name is on the cover, I'm always chasing the next story.

# ACKNOWLEDGMENTS

People think that the process of writing is solitary. That's not the case for me. I have help from so many people it would be hard to acknowledge everyone, but I'll give it a try.

The support and inspiration I get from my writer's groups is incalculable. The Vancouver Writers Social Group opens my mind to other ways of telling a story. The Royal City Literary Arts Society gives me the opportunity to meet and share with other writers who have more knowledge than I do. The Other 11 Months group is where I learn about getting the words on the page. And my critique group who helps me find the best parts of the story I want to tell. Thanks to all of the members of these great groups.

Last of all, but definitely a huge part of the process, my beta readers. These are the people who love stories and are willing, and more than able, to tell me if my finished story is ready for you, my readers.